TURN BACK TOMORROW

A Deliciously Indelicate Gambol Through Space and Time

Tim Schaefer

Also by Tim Schaefer

Darwin's Moon
(A Memoir of Pain and Glory in Poetry and Prose)

Last Tango in Timbuktu (Selected Stories and Poems)

Cover design by John Connolly

Virgin River Press
Virgriver77@gmail.com

For Terry Southern and Mason Hoffenberg,
who kept me up deep into the night, turning those pages.

Bein' lost is worth the comin' home.

-- Neil Diamond

One

Reno gazed up at the luminescent disc in the sky. A full moon would be good for the journey ahead—a long walk to... where? Well, hell—there was a reason why he was out here on this strip of asphalt in the desert and he would remember it momentarily.

Shit!

The moon. The sky. A white light. The images came flooding back. Incredible.

Impossible. But seemingly so real. He'd been gliding down the road in his cherry red '66 Mustang convertible with a groupie known as "Jack Off Jackie." She'd chosen the moniker herself, lamenting that none of the guys thought she was good enough to bang, but they'd allow her to whip the ol' weenie now and then.

 Her hand-always seemed to be stuck inside somebody's jeans—'fly-fishing" as she called it—to emerge with the squirming catch of the day. Only in this case, Reno, felt she was carrying the metaphor too far when she started whomping the head of his slippery eel against the steering wheel—pretending to kill it. Which she almost did before settling into a steady piston-like rhythm which soon became too much for him to bear. He pulled off onto a dirt road and cut the motor to allow her to finish the job—preferring that to weaving all over the road like a late night drunk. He'd suggested they step out of the car so she could milk him underneath the Milky Way, instead of on his new bucket seat covers.

Then, without warning, came the stab of light from a craft hovering directly overhead. At first he thought it must be a police helicopter, but he quickly discarded that idea when he felt himself being sucked away from the car by some unseen force. Then Jackie screaming, "Ohmygod what is HAPPENING? No, Reno... NO!" She unconsciously tightened her grip on his shaft, creating a momentary standoff as he was pulled in two directions at once—stretched to the limit like a maxed out Mastercard—the force winning out, his whanger going THWACK as it slipped her grip and snapped back into place. Slowly, Reno was lifted into the craft, pants still down around his ankles as he got a last glimpse of Jackie standing dumbfounded, mouth agape, fingers still curved into the loose fist which had primed his pump only moments ago.

He must have blacked out because the next thing he remembered was looking up into those EYES. He tried to bolt but realized that he was strapped onto some kind of gurney. He glanced from face to face. There were five of them. Humanoid creatures. Surprisingly close to resembling the sketches he'd seen in magazines. The eyes, of course-- huge and black--stood out. And they were all Yul Brynner bald.

One of the aliens stepped forward. Reno sensed that this one was female—not by any distinguishing characteristics—but by some subtlety of manner (he of the highly trained eye). She seemed to be smiling at him. (In the following days, he would see a photo of Sinead O'Connor and say, THAT'S HER!). With a sudden move she seized his tool in a vice-like grip and he cried, "GODDAMMIT, BITCH! THAT AIN'T NO POGO STICK... THAT'S MY DICK!

With her free hand, the alien inserted a speculum type device into the narrow slit of his penis and moved her head in close for a better view. Curiosity satisfied, she began to work him like a squeeze bottle of mustard--a look of wonderment upon her face. To Reno's chagrin, he felt himself responding—becoming firm in her grip—the initial pain yielding to a sensation of pleasure, as the others gathered round to observe the experiment. He tried to hold back, knew that he couldn't, and in that moment realized that even for a rock musician, this was the weirdest sex he'd ever had.

She leaned in close to him again and he shot his load all over her shiny bald head.

Two

Dan Rivers checked his watch against the control room wall clock. The watch was six minutes fast. That was good. The inexpensive timepiece tended to gain a few seconds each day—which gave him a slight margin of error for making appointments and such. When it got too far out of line he'd set it back—but the idea was to forget that there was any discrepancy. If time was money, there was always a little something in the bank.

He squinted at the program log and tried to decipher what spots were scheduled for the next break. The log sheets were tinted with streaky brown stains, the upshot of this morning's visit from Stacy's boyfriend. Their relationship was going down the tubes, and the morning shouting match had climaxed with Bruno grabbing her coffee cup and slinging its contents onto the walls and the papers on her reception desk—not to mention her hair and blouse.

Dan punched a button and said, "Let's go to Tiffany on line three—you're on the air on KSUK."

The disembodied voice said, "Hi, it's Tiffany."

"Is there—an echo in here?"

"Dan, I've got this gross neighbor who oughta be arrested."

"Peeking in your windows?"

"No, he's out mowing his lawn—topless—and the guy has BREASTS. Bigger than mine! Talk about a double standard. I go out like that and the whole neighborhood would be in an uproar: When will this discrimination against women stop?"

Dan allowed his audible sigh to carry into the microphone, course through the transmitter tower outside the building, and stream into the atmosphere where, like magic, the exact same sound was reproduced in homes, cars, and offices throughout southern Arizona. "Get a grip, Tif," he said. "Now I know this may come as a shock to those who've been indoctrinated over the past several years to believe otherwise—but men and women are NOT THE SAME."

"But—"

"Whether it's fair or not, we men derived a pleasure and a satisfaction from the female breast at tender age. It nourished us, and it gave us something to hold onto in a scary world. We can't help it if there's still something we find to be absolutely fascinating about it. The world is going nuts because we've lost the ability to place things in their proper context. Turning people OFF—like this guy is doing—isn't normally to get you thrown in the pokey, but turning people ON, which is what YOU'D be under the same circumstances, would."

"But—"

"Sleep on it, Tiffany. You'll sit bolt upright in your bed at three o'clock in the morning, crack your skull on the headboard and shout, Wow, I get it!"

"This station sucks."

"Thank you."

Dan squinted at the brown stained log again. Ironically, the next spot to be played was for a hemorrhoid preparation.

* * *

Making his way down the-hall, Dan felt apprehensive about his upcoming meeting with Sydney Ulysses Kaplan, the owner, GM, and self-styled "Papa Doc" president-for-life of KSUK radio. Applying for call letters that matched his initials had seemed like a good idea to Sid thirty years ago, before the word "suck" had risen to its current plateau of prominence. *School sucks. The government sucks. The Bears STILL suck*! "This station sucks" had turned into a kind of backhanded compliment from the regular listeners, like a password that identifies you as a member of the inner circle. Rush Limbaugh had his ditto heads. Dan had his "suck heads."

Dan's was the only local show still running on the station. His ratings were fairly good, but revenues had been down recently. The other time slots were filled by hosts from a second-rate talk network out of Dallas (all the big name names were locked up by other stations). It was cheaper to put the network gabbers on as a package than to pay the individual salaries of several local hosts. The downside was that he'd sacrificed that sense of identification that local personalities would have felt with their audience, and vice-versa.

The network had a right-wing blowhard who railed on and on about Bill Clinton's indiscretions at a time when it was clear that no one cared anymore. Then there was the female psychic who could tell you all about yourself from the sound of your voice, but couldn't remember to wrap up her segments in time for the mandatory spot breaks, so she was always getting cut off in mid-sentence. And the two sports guys who always wanted to talk about baseball--right in the middle of football season.

"I can't sell the whole day based on your numbers alone," the old man had told Dan. "And these network clowns aren't doing us any favors." It was true. And with more and more stations hitting the airwaves in the market, the ratings pie was being divided -into progressively smaller slices, which made it more and difficult to convince potential advertisers that they'd be getting a good bang for their buck with KSUK.

Harold Dick, the station's sixty-six-year-old news director, came barreling around the corner and nearly broad sided Dan in his mad scramble to reach the newsroom by air time. Dick would sit back in his office, yammering on the phone and attending to personal affairs until the dramatic da da dum dum news theme played through his monitor, suddenly reminding him of why he was supposed to be there. Then he'd make the headlong dash .down the hall, streaming papers and debris in his wake.

The old man forbade him to use anything but his full name on the air, but Stacy at her reception desk would still field the occasional call that went something like:

"Is Harry Dick there?"

"Yes, he is," she would say.

"Oh, so he's hangin' out again, eh?" (Snicker, snort, wheeze.)

Stacy naturally liked to give everyone the benefit of the doubt, so she fell for it every time.

Dan waited while his boss took care of business in the private bathroom adjoining his office. He looked around the room. Sid Kaplan's whole life was represented here. The framed award citations from the Kiwanis Club and other civic organizations. The tennis trophies he'd garnered as a much younger man. The family portrait with his wife and three kids—all girls. Sid had forbidden his air staff to cross the line into the kind of "frank" topics that Dan was now delving into on the air until each of his daughters was grown and out of the house. But Sid was a businessman as well as a doting father; and now, with seemingly every air personality attempting to out shock or out gross the other and grab the lion's share of listeners, Sid understood that the bland approach would no longer cut it.

When the small talk was finished, Sid looked Dan in the eye, and with a pained expression said, "You're well aware of our financial condition. I've fought to keep our heads above water, Dan—you don't know the half of it. But there comes a time when... oh, hell... I've agreed in principle to sell the station to Mike Fallon in a few weeks. Unless, of course, some kind of miracle is effected."

"Balls!" Dan exclaimed. He knew what Mike Fallon was about. The head honcho of Infomerzion Broadcasting—a national chain of stations he'd inherited from his business tycoon father--Fallon was the king of infomercial radio. He didn't give a damn about ratings— didn't need to. His modus operandi was to give a slot to every looney tunes preacher and snake oil salesman that would buy the air time and let them make their pitch to the public. It didn't matter to Fallon if anyone was listening or not, as long as his gang of eccentrics and egocentrics—and every town has them—paid cash on the barrelhead. Most of them were in love with the sound of their own voices.

"So that's all you're going to say, Dan... BALLS?"

Dan thought for a moment. 'NUTS!" he said.

Three

Reno was relieved to be riding instead of walking, even though it was a dilapidated VW bus chugging along at 45 miles per hour, which seemed to be its top speed. The driver, whose name was Derek, had spotted him moving erratically along the shoulder of the road. He'd stopped and said, "Hop in, bro—always room for one more."

Derek was a string bean with stringy shoulder length hair and Buddy Holly glasses. When he reached down into the crotch of his jeans and said, "Awright, come out of there you little devil," Reno figured he might have to bail out on the guy. Then Derek produced the flask of whiskey that had been tucked away, offered the bottle to Reno and said, "Be my guest." Reno politely declined.

It didn't occur to him that other passengers were on board until a head popped from underneath a blanket in back and said something in Spanish that Reno didn't understand. In short order the vehicle, headed north on 1-19 between Nogales and Tucson, veered off the highway, made a few turns, and ended up scattering dust on a gravel road.

By now Reno was trying to assess what kind of bunch he'd fallen in with. He wanted to find his car, and he wanted to locate Jackie, who likely would be behind the wheel. He pictured her speeding down the highway, weaving all over the road—one hand on the wheel and the other already inside some other guy's pants.

Derek's hand slithered inside his own jeans, securing the flask in its hiding place.

"Liquid courage," he said. "Don't want my friends back there to-be askin' for any... only so much to go around."

The old bus pulled to the side of the road and there was an immediate flurry of activity in the rear. One by one they piled out of the vehicle. There were eight of them, all Mexicans. Mostly young guys in their twenties, and one middle-aged couple with a raving beauty of a daughter, about sixteen. She wore a full length peasant dress. Her long dark hair glistened in the moonlight. Everyone murmured in Spanish, a language that Reno comprehended only selectively—slang words, mostly.

The teenage beauty eyed Reno in a way that told him she thought he was pretty. Most of the girls thought he was pretty. Reno Vegas, lead singer of one of Tucson's hottest rock bands—The Electric Grandmas. This little honey, though, was obviously more cherry than his Mustang. Then, to his surprise, he watched as she squatted by the side of the road—somewhat demurely with her long dress ballooning around her—and took a piss.

Farm out, man, he said to himself.

Derek took a last pull of hooch and tossed the empty bottle over a barbed wire fence. It made a dull tinkling sound as it hit the ground. He sidled up to Reno and said, "I'm gonna tell you something 'cause you look like an okay dude." He motioned toward the others. "This here group I got with me... they's a bunch of ALIENS."

Reno, still reeling from his abduction ordeal, eyed the man warily. "What KIND of aliens?" he said.

Derek laughed. Then he belched. The belch caused a chain reaction and he farted a split second later. "Got me a little international transport business. Lots of 'em want-to be on this side of the border before the end of the world hits, for some reason. Can't believe we're just over two months away." He did a little pirouette and chanted, "Y2K—two months away... Y2K—two months away."

"Y2K?" Reno queried. "That stand for something in particular?"

Derek did a double take. He pursed his lips and gave Reno the once over, as if this were the first time he'd laid eyes on the wayfaring stranger. He hadn't seen anyone decked out in bellbottoms for longer than he could remember. "I know you can't be serious, boy—but it's creepin' me out the way you LOOK so serious. You been hidin' out in a damn cave or what?"

Reno raised his arm slowly and extended a finger skyward. Both of them were now thoroughly confused.

Derek belched again. "I'm talkin' about the impending turn of the century disaster," he said. "The year 2000—all the computers are going to fail. It'll be total chaos!"

Reno shook his head as if to clear his brain. "Computers? Two thousand? That's thirty years from now!"

Derek waved his hand in front the stranger's face. "What year is it?" he said.

"It's Nineteen-sixty-nine. Last time I checked."

"Hhaaww... I may be a little fucked up, but I sure as hell know it ain't no nineteen and sixty nine... it's nineteen and NINETY NINE, boy!"

Reno stared at him for a long moment. "Oh... shit," he said.

Four

Dressed in his all-purpose work and play uniform of jeans, sneakers, and baggy sweatshirt, Dan lay sprawled in front of the TV. At least he didn't have to dress down at home to be comfortable. Radio being a medium of the imagination, Dan knew that some of his listeners would picture him outfitted in a coat and tie, while others might imagine him naked. He figured the way he dressed was kind of a happy medium between the two.

This was a night for eating popcorn and getting sloshed. The culinary experts of the world would never tell you that popcorn is compatible with red wine. That's something only a person with an open mind—or little left to lose--might discover. Every other mouthful, he'd take a kernel and toss it to his jack terrier, Harvey (named after legendary broadcaster Paul Harvey), who'd shag it on the fly nine out of ten times. Harv would then sit, ears erect, patient but focused, waiting for the next chance.

Dan never understood why certain things were done in prescribed ways. Like those same dead presidents' mugs on all of the currency. Why not Joe DiMaggio, or Elvis? Contemporary heroes that people could identify with. Half the Americans alive today couldn't name another pre-twentieth century president other than Washington or Lincoln anyway.

He picked up the remote and flipped through the channels with a random but deliberate vengeance. Mike Fallon was an asshole alright, and like a newly installed president with his own preconceived list of appointees, he'd come in and clean house at the station. Everybody out on their ear. Thinking about it, he was almost sadder for the rest of them than he was for himself. Especially Stacy. She was a good kid in a bad relationship, and now this.

He let up on the remote and it locked in on one of those interminably bubbly female voice-overs for a supermarket chain. The camera panned the meat and produce while she rattled on—no interpretation of the copy, just nonstop effervescence, as if she were on the verge of breaking into a number from *The Sound of Music*—as if the mere thought of T-bone steaks got her hot. Somewhere along the way, someone had told her that she would sound convincing if she smiled while reading certain phrases, so she figured if a little smiling was good, a whole lot of smiling would be better.

You could tell she thought she was good.

Why had HE never found a woman that excitable? He switched over to Wheel of Fortune. He was developing a fixation on Vanna White, but wasn't sure why. Here was a woman who had spent virtually her entire career as window dressing for a bunch of vowels and consonants. If God suddenly decreed that there were too many famous people in the world and the most superfluous of them had to go, Vanna would certainly be at the head of the line. And yet, she was beautiful, and if anything, seemed to be getting sexier with age. (He still possessed the May, 1987 issue of *Playboy*—the one with a young, bare-butted Vanna on the cover... and inside, those delectable hooters peeping through a transparent nightie. He also had the Madonna issue, but had gotten bored with that one rather quickly.)

But the days of the Vanna lookalikes were over, and he knew it. He was still a good looking man. Just over six feet and with most of his hair intact, though noticeably graying at the temples. A woman once told him he looked like an "old college boy." He didn't know whether to be flattered or offended by the remark.

At fifty-four, most of the women he found attractive thought he'd make a good match for their mothers. What was available in his age bracket, though, had too many battle scars. And the ones he'd dated were hardened and fickle. There was a reason why all-the-good-ones-are-taken was a popular cliché. You get to a certain age and you're still floating around out there—it says something about your ability to make a go of a relationship. As soon as that thought crossed his mind, Dan realized that he was describing himself as well.

It was during such times that he thought of Maya, then wished he hadn't.

The alcohol did its job and he drifted off. Harv helped himself to the popcorn and lapped up a little of the wine remaining in the glass to wash it down. In his dream, Dan lugged a briefcase loaded with thousand dollar bills into the radio station and plopped it onto Sid Kaplan's desk. "Our troubles are over!" he announced.
When he opened the case, all the bills had Vanna White's picture on them.

Five

He'd been strolling along the beach--grooving on the sun, the sand, the bikinis. A twenty-one year-old stud, living and working in a resort area where each week brings a new crop of heat-seeking misses. He had the world by the balls—but, like most, he wouldn't grasp that until he looked back upon it from some distant vantage point in the future.

It wasn't all innate charm. He discovered this when one of his imminent conquests came clean and admitted she'd do things on vacation she'd never dream of doing back in Buffalo—where she had a "reputation" to maintain. So that was what separated the nice girls from the sluts: location... location... location.

It was his first great epiphany.

He took note of the young woman he would come to know as Maya lying there, greased up like the bottom of a pie tin and baking to a nice golden brown in the sun—her ash blonde hair turning lighter by the minute. She was worthy of another look, he decided, so he tried to be cool, whistling some inane tune. Then he caught himself. One could put too much effort into being nonchalant. On the return pass, she caught him by surprise when she sat up and said, "Hello, Mister Rivers."

He was the house deejay at this funky beach side club in a place called the Dive Rite Inn. Apparently, she'd observed him spinning the tunes and tossing out wisecracks as the couples got down and dirty on the dance floor. Nothing like being in the public eye to pave the way for a private encounter.

That evening, a candle flame twitched in a red vase in the middle of the table, illuminating their faces with a soft glow. He'd drained a couple glasses of wine, getting buzzed too quickly as he tried to think of the right questions to ask about her life. Being a cheap drunk had its advantages—mainly, that it was cheaper to get drunk. It also had some disadvantages. He ordered another glass, knocked it over, and watched helplessly as the liquid turned into a waterfall cascading over the table's edge and into Maya's lap.

She jumped up, looked down at the large wet spot on her dress and said, "I can't believe an AMERICAN would do such a thing!"

He was mortified. His cover as a gentleman blown, she would now think of him as just another slob who couldn't hold his liquor. But what the hell did being an American have to do with it? Turned out she was on the return leg from a swing down to San Juan, where she found the blitzkrieg approach to romance employed by some of the local males not to her liking.

They rode back to her hotel in silence. When they reached her door he knew there was nothing to lose, so he said, "Don't suppose I'll be able to get into your pants now." He steeled himself for her reaction, figuring that it might hurt.

Instead, she gave him a cockeyed look and said, "You're a real turd, aren't you?"

He saw that the liquor had caught up with her as well, so he pressed his advantage and said—in a film noir voice—"Come in and I'll show you my etchings."

"Uh... it's MY room, you idiot!" She giggled then, and that's when he knew he had her.

Inside, she protested valiantly, trying to explain that she wasn't a first nighter—first to convince him—then so that she'd believe it herself. She was still protesting when he removed her blouse, and then the bra. She said they were rushing things. "You got me drunk, you scheming bastard... now you know I'm vulnerable, so you're taking advantage."

He took her from behind, on all fours down on the carpet. She was still complaining, but now it was only when he stopped to catch his breath. Not wanting to assume she was on the pill, he would prove that he was indeed a gentleman by pulling out when his release was imminent--peppering her lower back with his seed.

She looked back at him and said, "That's the second time you've spilled on me tonight."

Six

Reno heard the door slam and knew that his roommate was home. He was concentrating on the TV, so he didn't look up.

Derek joined him on the sofa. "Well, what did ye learn today, my boy?" he said.

"Weirdness all over the place, man."

"Jerry Springer, right?"

"And I'm trying to figure out why shaved heads are considered attractive."

Derek removed his glasses and rubbed the lenses with a patch of his shirt. "Well, you've got your skinheads—not attractive to most women. You've got to differentiate them from your athletes, who ARE, even though they may look the same to the uninitiated eye. It's the subtleties you've still got to pick up on. You'll get there."

Reno, grateful that Derek had taken him under his wing, had been camped out in front of his new mentor's television for the past two weeks. It would be the primary tool in his reorientation program. It was good to just lay about for a while. There had been that wild ride (his second of the evening) through the desert. The stab of headlights. Derek fearing the Border Patrol was on their tail. Some of the illegals made it back into the van. Some of them didn't. They'd be all right, though. Find their way to somewhere. It wasn't summer—that was the main thing. No way Derek would leave those people alone in the desert in the summer, where the heat could sap the fluids from your body so quickly, you wouldn't stand a chance.

He was an alright guy.

Reno took a pull off of his cold one and continued excitedly. "I'm trying to put my finger on it, man. It's like, we thought the peace and love thing would last. Deepen, you know. Age of Aquarius and all that."

Derek examined his glasses from both angles. "Yuh...well, after the war there was disco... then Ronald Reagan..."

"Things seem to have gotten... *nastier* in a way. Like this thing where people pull off along the road and beat the livin' crap out of each other with baseball bats and tire irons."

"Road rage. Yeah, I guess it IS weird. Thing is, we've kinda become numb to it. That and a lot of other stuff. It's part of who we are now—there ain't no goin' back."

Derek went to the fridge and got himself a cold brew. He rejoined Reno and said, "Now, you should know about the new rules of engagement."

"You mean like, to be married?"

"No, boy—I'm talkin' about how you can and cannot approach a woman! Used to be if you asked a gal out on a date and she said no, you could come 'round and ask her again. Then you could send her flowers, and maybe you could get in with her friends and have them put in a good word for you, and all manner of strategy—tryin' to break down her defenses so that she'd eventually say yes."

"You can't do that anymore? Bummer."

"NO--YOU CAN'T! Remember this—no means NO! Least that's what I read and hear about on them TV talk shows."

"I didn't know too many of 'em that ever said no."

"I'll ignore that. Listen, you can git your ass in a sling for what they call *sexual harassment*. The more serious side of that is called stalking."

"But perseverance—that used to be a good thing."

Derek popped the top on his brew. "Here's a quiz. You walk into an elevator, and the only person inside there is a beautiful woman who is totally, one hundred per cent nekkid... not wearing a stitch! The door closes and it's just the two of you in there. Now, what you gonna do?"

"Uh... we'll share a doobie... and when we're totally wasted, I'll stop the elevator between floors and we'll make it like rabbits."

"WRONG! You ain't gonna do nothin'! You're gonna say, 'Nice day out, ma'am,' and that's it."

"I KNOW you're goofin' on me now."

"You cannot do or say anything of a sexual nature to that woman, even though her lovely titties may be damn near poking you in the face, and that beautiful shrubbery betwixt her legs is a sproutin' like a Chia Pet."

"Bummer."

"We men are no longer the conquerors--conking them females on the head with a club and draggin' 'em back by the hair to our cave. Our job is to know our place and to stay in it... and to come when we're called."

"Geez... the world HAS gone crazy."

Derek shrugged, then got up and retrieved a plastic bag he'd set down on the kitchen table when he came in. He produced two pairs of jeans and a couple of shirts. "You've been wearin' my stuff long enough, so here's the humble beginnings of your new fall wardrobe."

"Farm out!"

"Uh... I thought the phrase back then was 'FAR OUT.'"

"Yeah, but then all the non-hippies were saying it too. So we had to change it. Always had to stay ahead of the curve. "

Being instantly catapulted thirty years into the future would present a whole new set of problems for anyone, and Reno was grateful to have Derek as his tour guide, interpreting the road signs along the way. Now it occurred to him that maybe he had something to teach this new generation as well.

He flashed back to that first night they had sized each other up, each of them thinking that the other might be a nut case, until Derek got the idea of comparing driver's licenses. They looked at the issuance and expiration dates. After that, there was no doubt in either of their minds as to what had happened.

What remained was the question of WHY? Those crazy alien peckerheads in that ship—had they purposely dumped him off at the cusp of the next century, or was it a miscalculation of some kind? Would he ever be able to go back? Would he want to go back? He'd been to places in his mind on that last acid trip--places that were at least as scary as this. Still, the changes in the world were mind blowing.

What REALLY floored him was learning that while the Beatles had broken up in 1970, the Stones were still out there rockin'.

Seven

"Sorry I can't give you more to go on, Dan," said Jack Davis from a thousand plus miles away. "The guy would just be around—but if he ever said two words to me, I don't remember 'em."

Dan had worked with Jack Davis a long time ago at a station in Missouri. One day, Davis was conducting a long running phone conversation with his girlfriend while he was on the air. It was grab a record, slap it on the turntable, say a few words into the mike, and get back to the cozy confab. He became increasingly distracted, and at some point carelessly grabbed the nearest album within reach without looking at it and cued the needle to the first cut. The song that played was the Mormon Tabernacle Choir singing "Silent Night" That turkey might have flown had it still been December, but unfortunately for Davis, it was the middle of February. The manager was listening. Jack got the boot.

A couple of months later, somebody blew up the station's transmitter tower. Davis—among others—had been questioned by the authorities, but they couldn't pin anything on him. Dan hadn't seen hide nor hair of him since, though he rightly assumed that the man had continued to reside in the same area--and one of the advantages of the internet was that you could look up anybody with a published phone number.

During his not so illustrious career, J.D. had also worked with Mike Fallon, back when the latter was getting his feet wet at one of his father's stations. "There was one thing, though, if you're looking for some dirt on this guy," Davis continued. "There was a rumor going around that he had the hots for the receptionist—name-of Maureen, or Doreen—something like that. Been a long time, you know."

"Really!" Dan felt like the guy whose horse has just rallied from dead last to take the lead down the stretch.

He was porking her, if the story was to be believed. Married guy like that. Can't confirm anything, though."

"This chickie have a last name?"

"Hell, it's been twenty years, Dan. The memory fades."

The horse faded badly as well.

"Don't imagine she'd still be working there."

"You know anybody that's worked at the same station for twenty years?"

The nag broke down. Dan emitted a sigh of resignation, but he didn't want the call to be a total loss. "Just one more thing, Jack—I've only been wondering about it for all this time. Did you do it?"

Davis laughed. He knew what his old associate was referring to.

"Come on, you know all secrets die with me."

"All I'm gonna say is—be careful when you're playing with dynamite, Dan."

Eight

Friday was Ask Any Question Day on Dan's show. Listeners would call in, and no matter how ridiculous, far-fetched, or idiotic the queries might be, he would counter with some sort of response.

The average male talk show host was an arrogant, tough-talking jerk who seemed to delight in belittling his callers. Put him on the street and he's likely just another overweight slob who couldn't punch his way out of a paper bag. But with the power of the microphone he is God. A metaphor for the modern dysfunctional male that modern dysfunctional females complain about. Hook up with him and you'll dangle at the end of his line. He'll manipulate you. Turn your own ideas against you if he can. He always has the last word—and in the end, you're the one who gets dumped. Dan just had to laugh at that type of posturing. Hipness, wit, sarcasm—they all had their place—but *unmitigated asshole* was not a label he cared to cultivate. Thus, Ask Any Question Day was a way of catering to the audience to repay them for their loyalty.

"How tall was John Wayne?" the caller asked.

"Shorter than most people thought. Line two... Sherry."

"Wow, man... did you see... the sun?" Her voice sounded like a 45 rpm record being played at a slower speed.

"I don't normally look directly at the sun, Sherry."

"Well, it's all red... and it looks like it's on fire. You think that means anything?"

"Here's the breaking news—and some of our listeners may already be on to this—the sun IS on fire! This discovery was made by that renowned scientist Jerry Lee Lewis back in the fifties—and GOODNESS GRACIOUS, Sherry, stop staring at the damn thing."

"Uh... okay."

"Line three—let's say hello to Gretchen."

"Good morning, Mister Rivers. It's a pleasure to talk to you at last."

Silky, sexy voice. Dan knew the percentages. That kind of voice was normally the hallmark of the dumpy, desperate groupie. Only guys who had met lots of women over the phone—such as radio personalities—were hip to this phenomenon. Normally, the outstanding ones didn't sound like anything special. Still, one could dream.

"Since anything goes, let me ask you this," Gretchen continued. "If you and your sister were stranded on a deserted island, with no chance of returning to civilization... would you have sex with her?"

"No way."

"And why not?"

"You haven't seen my sister. Now, if she looked like Kim Basinger..."

"I see. How about this—would you pull the wings off a butterfly for a thousand dollars?"

"No."

"Make it a million, then. If not for yourself, think of the charities that could benefit from that money—the homeless, starving people."

"Situational ethics, eh? Well, I'm not buying it, Gretchen. You don't create something good by starting from a place of evil. Have you heard of 'The Butterfly Effect?' The bad karma of callously destroying something beautiful would follow that money, wherever it was bound. And so, the answer is no. Not for a million dollars. Not in a million years."

"Very interesting, Mister Rivers," she said after a brief pause. Despite his instincts, there was something compelling about Gretchen that made him want to continue—in person. He signaled to Rick, his twenty-something call screener, to keep her on the line while he segued into a spot break.

Nine

Out in the desert, the coyotes started to sing. It began with a solo, then one by one the others joined in. Cletus Moore peered through the window of his cabin. How far out was he? Out where the hoot owls fuck the chickens, he was fond of saying (and that's about as far out as you can get). It was after midnight, but the desert was coming alive. The wind picked up, and all around, the palo verde, mesquite, and ironwood trees were swaying to the feral harmonics.

Cletus scooped a last bite of chili into his mouth and wiped his beard with his shirtsleeve. There was chili sauce in his beard. There was spaghetti sauce in his beard—from two weeks ago. There was beer, and wine that was still aging. And snot. There were even a couple of dead flies decomposing in there. You think Cletus Moore cared? No. He had bigger things on his mind.

He pushed open the creaky cabin door and stepped outside, where *billions and billions* of stars were draped across the firmament, as if they'd been glued to the top of the Metrodome in Minneapolis, which was where Cletus was from.

A hundred yards away the alien craft, its ring of multi-colored lights ablaze, descended from the sky—easing down onto the landing pad that Cletus himself had prepared.

His visitors were arriving.

Ten

Gretchen turned out to be the exception that proves the rule. She had an Asian look about her, and Dan was partial to such women, though he'd never actually been intimate with one. She was one of those types who didn't betray their age—could have been anywhere between twenty-five and forty—light skinned, with straight shoulder-length hair and bangs that cut an even swath across her forehead. Her hair was the color of a hearse, which seemed appropriate for such a drop-dead looker. He didn't have to think terribly long or hard to convince himself that she was the finest thing he'd ever laid eyes on. Which immediately set him to wondering what she was doing having drinks with *him* in a downtown bar.

She sipped her Margarita primly and gave him a shy smile. "Your responses to my questions over the air were quite intriguing, Mister Rivers."

"Don't get the wrong impression," he said. "I'm no saint and I've got no holier-than-thou attitude, it's just that we seem to have too many back doors these days. Whatever happened to standing on principle?"

"Well said, Mister Rivers—however, when standing on anything we must be cautious not to smash it into the ground."

"You don't need to call me Mister Rivers."

"There's a certain amount of safety in formality."

He didn't mind parrying with her if it bought him more time to look into those eyes, which were probably her most striking feature, though it would be difficult to pick just one.

He had long since ceased spilling drinks upon his dates, and for this he was thankful. These days he was more likely to baptize himself—which he did, on the third gin and tonic.

She touched his arm and said, "Accidents happen. You should get out of those wet trousers, though."

"My place is a ways from here," he said.

"Mine's probably closer. I have a robe that you can wear."

He thought he was dreaming.

She lived in some fancy digs. Fireplace in the living room. Fireplaces in the bedrooms. He wondered if the bathrooms had them too.

He sat there in the borrowed robe while she hung his pants up somewhere to dry, and returned with a couple of drinks.

He eyed the glasses. "You're going to trust me with that while your own vestment is draped around my body?"

"Of course, Mister Rivers... and if I trust you, perhaps you'll trust me in return."

She wanted to tie him to the bed. Big four poster job. He'd be in her warm and capable hands. That's classic, he thought. Behind the demure exterior, likely as not, you'll find a deviant. He had her all figured out.

He remembered his mama warning about girls who might want to lash him to a bed--or was that just some nebulous admonition about not getting tied down too early in life? No matter. In for a penny—in for a guilder. And he would always kick himself if he let this one escape without a tussle. He'd play her game for a while, then she'd play his.

Gretchen dimmed the lights and put soft music on the stereo. Soon he was bound hand and foot with the robe still loosely draped around him. She asked him to playfully struggle to pull free, and when he almost did she tightened the knots more determinedly. All the way over to her place he had cultivated this big boner, and now it reared its head through the silken material, creating a miniature teepee effect.

He was waiting for her to get undressed when she poked her head out into the hall and gave some kind of signal. Then came the sudden, sick realization that the two of them were not alone.

Like something out of a Fellini movie, a naked three hundred pound sumo wrestler of a woman waddled into the bedroom, grinning from ear to ear.

"What the hell!" he gasped.

"This is my friend, Brigitta," Gretchen said. "Do me this BIG BIG favor of entertaining her for a while, and then it's back to you and me, baby."

The massive mountain of flesh lost no time in mounting him and thrusting her pelvis into his face, the huge thighs of cellulite flanking him on either side.

"NO!" he cried, trying to turn his face away. He struggled against his bonds to no avail. The robe fell away to reveal that he was rapidly becoming vertically challenged.

Gretchen sat gingerly on the side of the bed and gave his flagpole a squeeze.

There was some cream in her palm, and she rubbed it up and down the length of his shaft.

He felt torn between the exquisite feelings engendered by the beauty's grip (her hands *were* warm), and the disgust that swept over him as he gazed into the abysmal gorge of the beast.

"Everyone needs love, Mister Rivers," Gretchen cooed into his ear. "I'm quite sure a compassionate man such as yourself understands." She dug her long red fingernails into his flesh, delivering just enough pain to get the point across.

Brigitta lowered herself onto his face and started to grind.

Dan ate. He ate like a man from Sudan. He ate like a stray cat rooting around in a garbage can. He ate like…well, let's face it—like someone with a big fat pussy being shoved in his face and nowhere else to turn! It was apparent that she'd spritzed some sort of feminine deodorant into that mine shaft, but its sweet perfume scent didn't make his task any less odious.

After what seemed like an eternity, Brigitta positioned herself further down, hovering over his loins.

Gretchen took his head in her hands and turned his face so that he was staring into her eyes. He looked at her like a child who's just been told there's no Santa Claus—the taste of the bitter pill he had to swallow still rife upon his tongue. She slid her hand down over his chest and stomach and seized his mast again. She guided him into port, relinquishing her grip only when the docking had been completed.

The profligate pachyderm grunted—an unintelligible animal sound.

Dan tried to will himself to lose his erection, with no success. It felt like most of the blood in his body was concentrated in his penis. He wondered if Gretchen had slipped him some kind of aphrodisiac back at the bar. The irony was not lost, as he thought back to all those times he'd concentrated on baseball, and when that wouldn't do it—soccer---just to hold out a bit longer. He thought back to a mercy fuck he'd once given to an overweight chick that brought him homemade dinners when he worked the night shift. But this was way beyond that, and all he could do now was appeal for mercy himself

Brigitta rocked back and forth on top of him, snorting and grunting— her pudgy pumpkin face and close cropped white-blond hair evoking some ecstatic, deranged Nazi bitch in heat.

Gretchen knelt beside the bed and said, "What a wonderful, compassionate man you are, Mister Rivers."

She bit his ear for good measure.

Eleven

Reno Vegas (whose given name of Jerry Clarkson was infinitely less catchy) grew up in the small town of Eloy, Arizona. As a high school sophomore, he hung with a group of "hoods" who all looked like Fabian with their duck's asses, black leather jackets, and ever present ciggy butt dangling loosely from the lips. The only two things for a kid like that to do in Eloy were shooting pool and hanging out on the street corner making mildly suggestive comments as the girls passed by.

The local authorities regarded him as a punk, and one day, as he was loitering outside a bowling alley on league night, they invoked some archaic law about disgusting behavior and hauled him in for excavating his nose with his little finger. Word got around and he became a kind of curious celebrity. His notoriety snowballed when he wrote and sang an original composition entitled "I Enjoy Picking My Nose" (sung to the tune of "I Enjoy Being a Girl") in the high school talent show. That was, until the red-faced principal gave him the hook.

Having tasted stardom, and thirsting for more, he joined the school band and learned to play a mean trumpet. Hoodlum days a thing of the past, he surprised everyone and graduated. A year later, after dedicating himself to the guitar, he opted for the surfer look—growing his hair long and straight and letting it bleach out in the sun—and joined a rock group in Tucson called The Electric Grandmas. He became the group's lead singer, and adopted the moniker of Reno Vegas because "it was there." The group .garnered a dedicated local following--playing everything from psychedelic rock to country—and had just released its first album on a small but respected label.

The sky was the limit.

It was that very milestone in the band's history that Reno was celebrating on the fateful night that found him cruising down the highway, his young admirer with situation well in hand—oblivious to the enormous twist of fate that lay just around the bend.

And so, it was not a good time for Reno to lose his life. The one that he knew, that is. Holed up at Derek's place, he was developing a case of cabin fever. He wanted to burst through his shell and step out into the brave new world, albeit on wobbly legs.

There were still some things that he might never be able to grasp— such as the growing popularity of professional wrestling, or why the government had gone ballistic over the drug "problem," when the only problem he'd ever had was running out of them. But he would play along. Blend in. Get a haircut.

What he wanted to do first was find out about the band. Derek did some checking around and learned that Mooch, the bass player, frequented a bar in South Tucson called The Hell Hole. Reno figured they'd just march down there and find him.

Derek, slugging down a Pacifico, burped and said, "Hold on, buddy—you got to think this thing through. What's this guy gonna think when you come sashaying in there, still twenty-three, and he's in his fifties now? He'll drop dead from heart failure. When he recovers, he'll think you're some jackass who looks a lot like you, best as he can remember, who's trying to pull off some stunt. It's plain to see, my man...you can't be you anymore."

* * *

The Hell Hole, true to its name, wasn't much more than a hole in the wall, with murals of mounted cowboys chasing the Devil's herd—a bunch of snorting red-eyed cows—through the clouds as in the song "Riders in the Sky." It was an old western standard, and one the band had sometimes played as a lark—everyone sporting those Halloween devil horns atop their heads. When they'd turn the fog machine on, the patrons would go wild.

The first time the two of them trekked down there, Mooch didn't show. The next night they found him, sitting alone, save for one leathery Mexican cowboy ensconced down at the end of the bar. Piped in *Norteno* music had long since replaced the live bands that played there in the heyday of the place.

Mooch was barely recognizable—he'd been a strapping specimen in his youth, but time and booze had taken its toll, and now the man looked gaunt and frail. The unkind years had washed most of his hair down the shower drain.

Derek eased onto the adjacent stool and ordered a beer. Reno wore shades, a fake beard, and a baseball cap with his hair tucked up inside. He sat two stools down, though his heart ached to be beside his old confederate.

And because Derek was barely out of diapers when Reno's band was hot, he knew he looked too young to claim outright recognition, so a little ruse would be in order. "Hey pard," he said, looking askance at the man. "Weren't you in a band that used to play around here years ago... The Electric UNCLES or something like that?"

Mooch's eyes widened, aghast that anyone might remember him now. He turned and gazed at the stranger for a long moment. "Who the hell are you?" he said. "My long-lost cousin? I ain't got any money."

Derek laughed. "No man. It's just that my mother has this autographed picture of the band—she was a big fan, ya know—up on her mantle. I'd recognize you anywhere, even without the hair."

Mooch half-smiled then, and something akin to a gleam beaming through the haze that clouded his recollection of the past showed in his eye. It only lasted a moment. The muscles in his face sagged again. "Long time ago,' he said.

"Uh, whatever happened to that group?" Derek asked nonchalantly.

"Had a record. Did okay. Got us some name recognition. Follow up would have sent us straight to the top. But that was it. Lead singer up and disappeared off the face of the earth. Never found his body. This groupie claimed to be the last one to see him alive, but she went plum crazy afterward. Spent some time in the state hospital." Mooch drained the rest of his beer. Cleared his throat. "He had the charisma, that Reno did. Nobody could take his place. And then the negative publicity that followed...talk of a drug overdose... we played a few more gigs, but everyone knew it was over."

Two stools down, a tear traversed Reno's cheek.

Derek placed a consoling hand on Mooch's shoulder. "Anybody else from that group still around?"

The next night they checked out a place called The Rancid Ranch, an out of the way club near the industrial section of downtown Tucson. A sign at the entrance announced: *PEE ON YUR SISTER—tonight at 9.*

"What's that mean?" Reno asked.

Derek sniggered. "Must be the name of the group."

"Wow, and we thought Electric Grandmas was out there."

The band was playing when they went inside. Two young guys with closely cropped hair on guitar, a drummer with tattoos all over his face, and a female singer with long black hair. She wore heavy makeup that enhanced her lips and eyes.

Reno looked around. A large group of kids near the stage appeared to be dancing, but it wasn't like anything he'd ever witnessed.

He didn't know how they'd find Turtle in this melange. Mooch had mentioned that the former lead guitarist of Reno's old group was now managing a band that played here on Friday nights. Luckily, they didn't have to seek him out. Turtle spotted them--the two most out of place looking dudes in the club—and made his way over.

"Thought you guys might be lost," he said, proffering a hand to Derek. "I manage the band. They think I'm an old fart, but they're sharp enough to know that I've been around and can get them bookings."

Reno thought Turtle had aged well. He combed his hair back behind his ears where it cascaded into free-form curlicues down the back of his neck, distracting from the patch of barren tundra on top. Unlike Mooch, he had laugh lines around his mouth and eyes. He was a little broader around the middle than back in the day. As he had ached to do with Mooch, Reno wanted to throw his arms around his old pard, but knew that he couldn't.

The band came out of a long, cacophonous instrumental bridge that sounded to Reno not so much like music as guitar abuse. Then, in a guttural, testosterone driven voice, the singer revealed that "she" wasn't a she at all: *I HATE YOU... I DON'T NEED YOU... FUCK YOU!* The lyrics, in their entirety, consisted of a steady repetition of those three phrases.

"You guys into the punk scene?" Turtle queried, not waiting for a reply. "Actually, you'd have to call them punk with a little goth and maybe some grunge—and some speed metal in there too. The group defies description."

Reno didn't disagree.

Derek said, "Uh, yeah... punk rock... that's the scene. Gotta keep up with the times."

Reno watched the kids, some wearing spiked dog collars, go at it in the mosh pit. Disguising his voice with a southern accent, he said, "Those kids are really knocking each other around. What are they mad about?"

Turtle looked at Reno in bemusement. His long and still lost friend had the same get up on he'd fooled Mooch with the night before. "Say, where you from, anyway?"

Derek jumped in. "Uh, my friend here's from the country. WAY out in the country."

Turtle laughed. "That's called slam dancing—they're not pissed at each other. It's just the thing to do at this kind of scene."

The three of them watched as a young girl was hoisted on top of the crowd and passed from the front to the rear on a sea of outstretched hands.

"Surfin' the wave," Turtle explained.

As if by prearranged signal, the hands that held the girl aloft allowed her to tumble to the floor, where she flopped around for a moment like a fish tossed into a rowboat.

"Some of the kids get a little bruised up," Turtle said. "It's like a badge of honor to them."

"Cool song," said Derek, trying to come off as cool in his own right.

"That's a Pee on Yur Sister original. It's called *Fuck You.* No, wait... I think it's called *I Hate You.*"

"Seems to fit either way," Derek said.

Turtle lowered his voice to a level of confidentiality. "Sounds like crap, doesn't it?"

Derek and Reno looked at each other sheepishly. "Yeah... crap." Derek said.

"Right on... crap." Reno admitted.

"But that's the whole point. Most of these bands want to produce the shittiest, most god-awful kinds of sounds imaginable—stuff that people really hate. The more the kids hate it, the more they love it, and the more popular the band becomes—get it?"

"Heh heh... SURE," chirped the two strangers in unison.

Turtle's eyes narrowed as he regarded Reno again. "You sure we haven't met somewhere before, man? Can't put my finger on it, but there's something familiar-"

"Uh, no—don't think so, man," Reno said.

"Maybe in another lifetime," Derek said.

Turtle laughed again. "Yeah...maybe that was it... another lifetime."

"I dunno if I can handle any more of this," Reno said as they pulled up to the ramshackle trailer where The Groupie Formerly Known as Jack-Off Jackie now resided.

Derek took a long pull off of his beer. "You remember that old movie, *It's a Wonderful Life?*"

"Yeah... Jimmy Stewart."

"You're doing the same trip, my boy. Discovering how the world turned out without you. You need to see this shit."

"Yeah, but Jimmy Stewart had that angel—what's his name—to guide him."

Derek belched, grinned, and waited for his passenger to see the similarity.

Reno shook his head.

They knocked on the door.

"Remember what I told you," Derek said. "Drop the 'farm out' and the 'right on' shit or you're going to give yourself away. Just use 'dude' when addressing people—that'll help."

"Women too?"

"Yeah, what the hell."

"Okay, yeah, dude. Right on."

Derek implied that they were detectives. Jackie had gotten used to the occasional police dick, refusing to let the old case die, coming around to pick her brain. What was left of it.

Reno had traded in his old disguise for one with a long beard that made him look like an alumnus of ZZ Top. Derek could pass for a certain type of dissipated rock musician himself. Inspecting the two of them, Jackie's heart began to flutter, just like in the old days.

Reno was appalled by what he saw... and smelled. Her scraggly hair was one shade of gray, her skin another. She had about three teeth left in her head. Below her tattered knee-length house frock, one spindly leg sheathed in a nylon, the other bare. The scent of urine hung in the air as if someone had splashed it on like perfume.

Resting on her sofa, Derek and Reno each felt a metal spring jabbing them in the butt.

Jackie, perched directly across from the men, gummed off the end of a cigar and spat it onto the floor, where it landed at Derek's feet. One of several cats, who did their part in contributing toward the rent by bringing home disgustingly dead lizards and mice (some of the half-eaten body parts were still strewn about), had hopped onto Reno's lap and was sticking its ass in his face. Detecting movement, the cat pounced onto the slobbery cigar bit and began to bat it about in a wild frenzy.

Derek did most of the talking. He was good at drawing people out. And so, Jackie puffed her cigar and told her sad tale. Of being the initial prime suspect in Reno's disappearance. Of nervous breakdowns. Of being pumped full of drugs during her stint in the looney bin. No one had believed her abduction story, but she would stick to it till her dying day.

The one person in the world who absolutely knew she wasn't full of shit couldn't afford to say anything. Not yet, anyway.

"Say, you guys don't look like cops," she said observantly as the men rose to depart.

"Uh, we're doing a little undercover work on the side," Derek countered.

They had nearly reached the van when she poked her head out the door and called to them. "Hey, you guys want I should jerk you off before you leave?"

"Thanks anyway," said Derek. "We'll handle it ourselves."

Twelve

Dan still cringed when he thought about it. Although mortified, he had not been able to control his purely physical response as the monstrous Brigitta had pumped him until she was plum full of his joy juice, grunting and snorting like a wild javelina throughout.

At some point, after Gretchen had untied his wrists, allowing him to free his legs and find his pants again--stumbling about and cursing a blue streak, the two of them had simply disappeared. Had he thought about it at the time, he would have searched the house for clues to their identities, but he wasn't going to hang around to see what further surprises might await (could there be MEN lurking about, licking their chops as well?). So he got out of Dodge while the getting was good.

He returned the next day in sunlight, a Louisville Slugger tucked discreetly behind his back, only to be greeted at the door by a benign looking couple in their sixties who said yes, a woman named Gretchen had been house sitting for them during their summer sabbatical in Wisconsin, and that her tenancy had expired as of last night. No, they didn't know much about her—she'd answered their classified ad, provided several references which they hadn't bothered to check out, being in a hurry to leave town, and... well, she'd seemed so disarmingly NICE. And proper.

In other words, she'd charmed the pants off of them as well.

He checked into every possibility he could think of. He revisited the bar where that whole crazy night got started. The waitress who'd served them remembered her—who wouldn't take note of such a stunning creature? But she didn't recall ever seeing the woman prior to that evening.

He buttonholed the board operators who worked the later shifts at the station. Oftentimes, women who were drawn to radio personalities were not averse to spreading the wealth to even the lowly board ops—the status equivalent of the roadie in the rock music world—the guy who, by virtue of his proximity to the scene, occasionally scores with groupies when the band members are already up to their asses in comely young lasses. None of them had encountered anyone who faintly resembled "Gretchen."

A week passed. Driving to work with the mystery woman still on his mind, Dan conceded that he was heading down a dead end. What to do—rent a billboard asking for information on an Asian psycho-bitch and her corpulent, sex-starved sidekick? Chalk it up to experience? No. Chalk up the blind date that doesn't go so well, but not this.

Thing is, he thought, if anyone should know better than to get involved with chicks you meet off the phone lines, that someone should be yours truly. Great bit for the airwaves, eh? Guess what folks, it's good news/bad news. The good news is ... I got laid. The bad news is... it was Bigfoot!

A song he liked popped into his head: "The Heart Never Learns." That was the gist of it, right? And though he fought to keep his thoughts from going there, the tape recorder in his mind rewound through time—taking him back to Maya.

* * *

They lived together in the Summer of Love— 1967. "Light My Fire" became an anthem, dominating the airwaves. But Maya was a throwback to a simpler time. She could sing, and she'd gained a foothold in the sunbelt by fronting a small jazz combo that played regular club gigs on the beach, and sometimes hired out for parties.

She was all over the place, from Billie Holiday to Leslie Gore's "You Don't Own Me"—the first real women's lib song—ahead of its time when it hit the charts in '64. And she did a Mae West impersonation that always wowed them at the end. Dan didn't have a clue as to where she'd absorbed all of that growing up in small town Iowa.

He did his rock radio show during the day, and his club deejay thing on Friday and Saturday nights. There were always temptations, like the fine looking chick who walked right up and, with nary a word, lowered her tube top to display a pair of nicely rounded breasts for his approval. But he remained true to Maya, collecting her after her last set, then walking along the beach together into the early morning hours. They'd bury their toes in the sand and gaze at the stars— bodies existing in one reality, their spirits in another. She spoke of retreating to a desert island where they could wander naked all day— regain that elusive sense of innocence she instinctively knew, despite the times, was disappearing from the world for good.

Once she found herself in a hotel room with two other women and some Major League baseball players who were in the area for spring training. Maya thought they were there just to meet the guys and maybe get some autographs. Anyway, that's what her girlfriend had said. The players thought the women were pros who were there to do some numbers on them. Maya ended up running down a hallway with one of the biggest names in baseball--a living legend-- in hot pursuit, wondering why she was acting so coy.

Another time she fell in with an outfit called The Children of Jesus. She was attracted to their joyful spirit—the way the long haired girls and guys would hold hands and sing and dance around in a circle. At nearly every meeting, the leader would read a letter he claimed he'd received from their nebulous guru, (an enigmatic type who lived in

Hawaii... or Timbuktu) but which he'd actually written himself—offering encouragement and spiritual advice, to the collective "oohs" and "ahhs" of the participants.

When Maya learned that one way the Children of Jesus recruited new blood was to have female members use their sexuality—in fact, whatever it took—to lure young guys into the group, she told them where to go (and it was the exact same place they seemed to be trying to avoid!) Still, until proven wrong, she gave everyone the benefit of the doubt. That was just who she was.

Dan could not—would not—for the sake of the fragile truce he'd established with his psyche that allowed him to continue with his life, go further into that realm of pain that might again cause him to question the reasons for his own existence.

Thirteen

Pulling into the station parking lot, Dan saw the white Mercedes parked beside Sid Kaplan's Oldsmobile and immediately smelled a rat.

Fallon was there.

Shit happens in threes, he recalled, and this was doo doo number two. Nothing to do but go inside and be as gracious as one could be to a man who's bent on taking away your livelihood.

Stacy appeared tight-lipped at her post near the door. Her eyes were puffy. It didn't take long to determine why. The wall behind the reception desk had that freshly wiped down look, indicating that Bruno had struck again. He had splattered, then split, only minutes ago.

She manufactured a smile and said, "Morning, Dan. Kaplan's in a meeting."

"Listen," Dan said in a fatherly tone, "either dump that loser boyfriend of yours or he's going to have to kick in for the coffee he's muraling our walls with."

"At least the old man didn't see it," she said, nodding toward Sid Kaplan's door. "They've been in there for over an hour."

Dan knew that Fallon would soon be receiving the nickel tour, which would allow him to size up the place, and that their itinerary would take them right past his office, and that an obligatory introduction would be in order. But that was all right. He wanted do some sizing up of his own.

Mike Fallon: Dark. Trim. Silk shirt. The predictable Wingtips. Hair slicked straight back and a little oily.

Unavoidable would be the "power handshake," that men filled with their own sense of self-importance—whether six foot five or five foot six—always proffered. The kind of grip normal guys would affect only when arm wrestling. When they met, Dan was prepared, determined to give it back measure for measure. Had the two of them squeezed any harder, there would have been the distinct sound of bones crunching. Fallon registered a look of half surprise.

Watching them, Sid Kaplan grimaced. He looked lost.

"I've heard your show," Fallon said. You do a good job. You'd think it would be more highly rated." His smile never wavered as he slid the knife in.

The old man directed Fallon down the hail before Dan could reply. Good move on his part. There they would find Harry Dick—feet propped up on the desk--jabbering away on the phone. He'd be the first casualty, no doubt, of a new administration.

Later, Dan observed Fallon chatting up Stacy, and recalled his conversation with Jack Davis.

Fourteen

Reno was, in a real sense, an alien himself, and the growing sense of "alienation" he felt—slinking around like some criminal, was taking its toll. And so Derek hit upon the idea of hauling him off to the one place where he would feel at home.

The abductees meeting was held on Monday nights in the back room of a metaphysical bookshop called The Awakening Dream.

A middle-aged redhead wearing a tube top stretching every fiber of its being to constrain her ample breasts said, "I'll go around the room and show you the scar on my wrist where the implant used to be. As many of you know, the aliens removed it the second time they took me."

When she got to Reno, she held her wrist close to his face like a salesperson touting samples of perfume. But all he could detect was the musky smell of her armpits.

A young guy sitting in the corner said, "I have a scar on my butt, if anyone..."

No takers.

The redhead said, "I turned up pregnant shortly after they took me. I was carrying a fetus that would have been a human/alien hybrid had it come to term. They live among us as we speak."

"Yeah," said the guy with the butt scar, "look at Michael Jackson."

Reno decided to speak. "I was abducted in the middle of a hand job in 1969 and catapulted thirty years into the future. I was born in 1945. I'm still only twenty three years old."

The room fell silent.

"He's a fake," a fat guy whispered to his wife.

"You're the first group of people I've told," Reno continued.

Tube Top Woman gave him a serious look and said, "Can you prove your identity? Would anyone around here validate you?"

Reno thought of Jackie, Turtle, and Mooch. "It's not as simple as all that. And I'm not ready to be carted off to the looney bin by telling the whole world."

"But think of what this means," she said. "You... me... everyone in this room... legitimized! No one rolling their eyes when we walk by, or sniggering behind our backs." She rose to her feet and crossed the room again to stand directly in front of the new guy, one imposing breast occupying the entire field of his vision like a globe suspended in space. "You OWE it to the world to step forward."

On her globe, Reno pictured North America, then Africa and the Middle East. From Nepal, the nipple protruded like Mount Everest.

Derek had made another run to the border and back. He'd always been low-key about it, but on days when he slept past noon, all Reno had to do was creep out to the van and check for empty hooch bottles to confirm his suspicions.

While Derek was dead to the world, Reno scanned the local radio dial. A mellifluous male voice said, "Welcome back to the Dan Rivers show on KSUK. Let's go to line three—Melissa, what's on your mind."

KAY-SUCK radio! Reno had to laugh. *Suck* was the in word now. He tried to think back to its 1969 counterpart--a word that dominated. A word that was bandied about wherever one went.

Peace.

That was it. How things have changed. Turmoil was a better word for what was going on now. His thoughts were in turmoil as well. Derek, had he been conscious, would have told him no way are you going public with this thing, man. But Tube Top Woman had stirred something inside him. It wasn't like he felt himself being swept along on the tide—it was more a sense of being thrashed in the irrepressible undertow of fate.

The fabled men of history had faced similar moments of decision. Truman and The Bomb. Kennedy and the Cuban missile crisis. Custer at Little Bighorn. (He didn't want to end up like the latter.)

He leafed through the phone book till he found the yellow pages heading for radio stations. He always felt he was destined for big things—he just never dreamed it would come down like this.

* * *

Dan had put some eccentrics on the air before. Like the lady who claimed Madonna was the reincarnation of the Virgin Mary. After all, think about her NAME. And there had been that song, "Like a Virgin." Well, the evidence was overwhelming!

And the colon hydrotherapist who wanted to do a live, on the air demonstration with Dan as the guinea pig so he could tell the listeners how much better (and presumably lighter) he felt afterward.

So when the call came in from a guy named Reno, laying out the basics of his fantastic tale and then claiming that he could 'PROVE it, Dan said what the hell. If nothing else it would generate some scuttlebutt for the show.

✱ ✱ ✱

At 8:05 on a Monday morning, Reno donned a pair of headphones, took a deep breath, and spoke into the mic: "My name is Reno Vegas and I disappeared from the face of the earth in October 1969. Everyone figured I'd been killed, but as your listeners can hear, and as you can see, Mister Rivers, I am still very much alive."

When Reno had finished his tale (being as delicate as possible about certain details of his abduction), Dan said, "There you have it, folks, now it's your turn. The lines are open. Is this man who claims to be Reno Vegas perpetrating a hoax, or is it just possible that he's for real?"

The phone lines lit up like Teddy Kennedy on the Fourth of July. A caller named Bill: "The guy's fulla crap." Click.

"Ask him what he's been smokin'," said Ned.

Then Ashley spoke in a smooth, relaxed voice. "Mister Vegas, you sound as though you're still confused as to the purpose of your abduction. From what you've described, it sounds like they extracted a sperm sample from you to be used for their human-alien breeding program."

Her statement struck a nerve. They'd covered a lot of ground in that meeting, and some of the things he'd heard from the other "abductees" seemed a bit far-fetched for even Reno to believe. But the hybrid thing kept popping up.

At the very moment that bulb lit up in Reno's brain, Dan flashed on his encounter with the two psycho-bitches. The hairs on the back of his neck woke up and danced around like they were on American Bandstand. Sure, anything was possible, but he had always felt that a logical explanation existed for most of the paranormal events that hit the news. Now, he had to admit, his interest was piqued.

"Mister Vegas—giving you the benefit of the doubt—you stated that you could PROVE your account of these events to be true. I'm asking you now to present that proof."

Reno dug into his shirt pocket and produced a newspaper clipping, yellowed with age. He carefully unfolded the fragment and held it-- pinched between two fingers—in front of Dan's face. The clipping, which had a faint musty smell to it, was from the Arizona Daily Star. It showed the date up in the right hand corner: October 21st 1969. The headline read: *POPULAR LOCAL MUSICIAN DISAPPEARS-- FOUL PLAY NOT RULED OUT.* A head shot photo appeared beneath it. The young man in the picture had longer hair but... by GOD! By holy livin' JESUS! This kid was a dead ringer--or more accurately, a live ringer—for the person in the photograph.

"Uh, ladies and gentlemen, I want to say that I don't believe my eyes. My rational mind tells me there must be some kind of trickery here, and certainty much can be done with cosmetic surgery... but I have to tell you that my guest this morning bears an UNCANNY resemblance to this photo of the missing Reno Vegas. And what sends a shiver down my spine is that... they appear to be the same age!"

Across town, Lawrence Milburn, Agent In Charge of the local FBI field office, who, in the course of protecting the national security of these United States, monitored talk radio shows on a regular basis to get a bead on potential terrorists, assassins, middle school students cutting class, and other subversives, jerked bolt upright in his chair. He picked up the phone and dialed a number he knew better than his own.

Meanwhile, Detective Hector Almorzado, who'd inherited the Reno Vegas case from the original investigator (now retired), the trail having long since grown cold; a case that was given attention only in the passing reflection of how long it had gone unsolved—cruised along Speedway Boulevard, punching in and out of the various radio frequencies on his dashboard dial. By random chance, his finger lingered long enough on 690 to hear the name he never expected to hear. He activated his lights and siren, gunned the engine and ran a red light, speeding toward the KSUK studios north of town.

Dan Rivers had been around a while. He knew about radio and he knew about radio groupies. Reno Vegas, in his relatively brief existence, knew about music and he knew about rock band groupies. Neither of them, however, was cognizant of the forces that had been awakened, the machinery now grinding into motion, bearing down on them as they spoke. And so neither of them did the prudent thing immediately.

Which would have been to run.

What they hadn't considered was that the government had already spent a good many taxpayer dollars in their campaign of disinformation to convince the public that every UFO sighting worldwide was nothing more exotic than a weather balloon. Ever since the Roswell incident back in 1947, they counted on your average Joe Six Pack, nodding off in front of the TV with a beer in his hand, not putting two and two together to deduce that if such an enormous number of weather balloons had actually been floating around up there all these years, the prognosticators would likely do better than to call for sunshine on a day when the rain comes down in buckets. The point being that the feds weren't going to let some upstart nose picker from Eloy, Arizona change the climate of ignorance in the country now.

Dan glanced out the side window. A car pulled into the lot. Then another, screeching to a halt. Through the front control room window he saw Stacy gesticulating wildly, trying to gain his attention. Out in the lot, more vehicles arrived. A woman wearing a nightgown jumped down from her pickup truck. Detective Almorzado bailed from his car and hit the ground running. Lawrence Milburn and three fellow FBI agents were right behind. The five of them pulled up to the station entrance in a dead heat.

Almorzado whipped out his badge and said, "You folks clear out of here—this is police business."

Milburn flashed his own badge and said, "Wrong! We're taking charge here."

Dan, shifting into full-scale emergency mode, spat into the mike, "This interview is concluded!" Ever the professional, he avoided dead air by punching up a CD that happened to be Lalo Schiffrin's "Mission Impossible Theme."

Reno bolted from the room, eyed Stacy and shouted, "Where's the back door?"

"Down the hall—first one on the right."

Reno ran. See Reno run. See Reno run fast. Halfway down the hall he turned and hollered, "Thanks—you've done the world a great service!"

The lawmen burst through the door, each trying to muscle the one beside him out of the way. A gaggle of curiosity seekers spilled in behind them.

"Where's Vegas?" Milburn barked at Stacy.

She shrugged and gave him two palms up, as if to say I'm just the ignorant slut who works here.

Dan moved to block the path to the hall. He introduced himself and said, "May I help you gentlemen?"

"We'd like a word with your guest," Detective Almorzado said.

Dan sized up the group. With his flat-top do, Almorzado was a throwback to the fifties. Milburn and his cohorts looked ill at ease in their coats and ties. You can put a gorilla into a suit, but all you get is a well-dressed gorilla. "You know you can't just barge in here and take over without a—"

"Where's the bathroom?" Milburn said in a flash of inspiration.

"Damn, I have to go too," said Almorzado.

"Yeah, WE have to go TOO," the other agents chimed in.

"You wouldn't deny us the courtesy of taking a dump, would you?" said Milburn as the entire assemblage pushed past the radio host and sprinted down the hall.

At that very moment, crack KSUK newsman Harry Dick woke with a start and thought he'd heard the news theme playing, which in fact, he did, but only in his dream. Scooping up a sheaf of papers, he scrambled out of his chair and broke into a dead run, barreling headlong toward the intersection of the north and west running hallways, where he would normally negotiate a hard right and crash land in his news chair just in time to flip open the mic and shift into his Walter Cronkite persona.

A fly parked on the wall near the middle of that L intersection was the only living entity that could see what was coming. It gazed upon the impending train wreck, magnified in the multiplicity of its eyes, and uttered the fly language equivalent of *SHEEE--ITTT* a second before Harry and the lawmen collided, the force of which sent all six of them sprawling, dazed and confused, with little cartoon birdies chirping and circling about their heads.

In the back lot, a white Camaro sat with its engine running. The driver beckoned to Reno as he burst into daylight. He recognized the flaming red hair.

It was Tube-Top Woman.

Reno tumbled into the passenger seat as she jerked the car into gear, tires screaming and spitting a hailstorm of rock and gravel against the side of the building. She blew through the gears like Steve McQueen in the chase scene from *Bullitt*, careening around corners and gunning it on the straightaway.

"I—I'm sorry, I don't think I got your name at the meeting," Reno shouted over the roar of the engine.

"It's Sondra," she shouted back. "And if I were you I'd make use of that seat belt—and scrunch down so it looks like I'm just some hot broad out for a joyride by herself."

Fifteen

They sat facing each other across Dan's desk. "First, I'd like to apologize for the way my men and I handled things yesterday." Agent Milburn, who had phoned earlier saying he wanted to "clear the air," was considerably more subdued. Perhaps the large lopsided bandage over his left eye had something to do with it. "We were heavy-handed and overstepped our bounds," he continued, milking his mea culpa for another moment before turning to the real purpose of his visit—and Dan knew as well as he it wasn't self-effacement.

The agent cleared his throat. "Like your job, Mister Rivers?"

"Mostly," Dan said.

"Powerful medium, isn't it?"

Dan nodded.

Milburn had a strained look about him when he spoke, as if he were not only dealing with matters of grave national concern, but constipation as well. "Think of the stir your little ol' radio program caused, then think about what would happen on a national scale if yesterday's show had been broadcast across the country. Think of the consequences."

"Don't tell me... 'War of the Worlds' all over again."

Milburn's head dropped onto his chest and he seemed to be contemplating his navel. For a moment, it appeared as though he'd fallen asleep. Dan stared, not knowing what to do. He watched the second hand on his wall clock make one full revolution. Then, suddenly, the man jerked into motion as if someone had stuck a quarter in his ass. "CHAOS!" he shouted. "ANARCHY... RIOTING IN THE STREETS... LOOTING!"

"Let's not forget pillaging. Did you just fall asleep a minute ago?"

Milburn returned a sheepish look. "Sorry about that, my friend. Been keeping some late hours."

"I think you'd better just come out with it."

The agent pulled his chair closer to the desk. "Tell me straight, Rivers... was it him?"

"Looked like the same guy."

"I can't tell you what to do, but--"

"That's right because that would be censorship, and we have something known as free speech in this country—so BUT what?

"If you care about your country—if you have a drop of patriotic blood—the second thoughts you'll have about your eyesight on tomorrow's program will cause you to conclude the guy was a fake... like, uh... an ELVIS impersonator."

Dan assessed the situation. If he played the whole thing down, it might take the heat off Reno. Hell, he didn't even know the guy, but one thing was certain—he was a marked man and Dan was partially responsible. Something, however, told him it was already too late. Pandora's box was agape and she, lying there like the whore she was, leered at him from atop a four poster bed.

Milburn would be going after the kid no matter what. And that detective, you think he wasn't already out there scouring the city, using all his resources to bring this guy in? Reno had made the call to go public because he knew, as Dan was beginning to understand, that the story was bigger than himself. Bigger than anyone and everyone.

"The American people are not children," Dan said, "even though our government—your employer—regards them as such."

"You're wrong, Rivers. They're just like children—too inquisitive for their own good. Don't you understand what would be compromised if everything were open and above board? Dammit, we're talking national security here!"

Dan brought his index finger to his lips and gazed into an imaginary distance. "Let's say that the government has known all along that these extra-terrestrials exist. And let's say that's not the half of it. Let's say that by mutual cooperation, we've learned how to manufacture these flying saucers, and that some of the sightings, like those lights over Phoenix that were witnessed by a whole shitload of people, and which were captured on videotape and shown on the ten o'clock news—let's say that some of them are our own flyboys taking her out for a spin so to speak. You could see why the powers that be would have a vested interest in convincing people they didn't actually see what they saw."

Milburn shook his head. "I don't have any Top Secret clearances. I'm just a good soldier, following along with the program--like YOU'LL do if you know what's..."

Dan gaped, incredulous. Agent Milburn had fallen asleep again.

Sixteen

Reno collapsed onto Sondra's couch. The events of the last few hours swirled around in his head. Before going to the radio station, he'd hit upon the idea of revealing himself to Jackie, sensing correctly that that she would possess a clipping with his picture on it. When he arrived back at her place on his own, she hugged him and wept like a baby. "Oh Reno, it's you... it's really you! Now they will see I wasn't crazy after all," she cried, gumming the wrong end of a cigar in her mouth.

But it wasn't going to be that easy. He'd told Jackie of his plan to go public on the Dan Rivers Show, and if all hell broke loose the first place they'd look for him would likely be her squalid abode. But he would see her again, that much he promised. In the meantime, her lips were to be sealed. It also wouldn't hurt if she acted just a little nuttier than before, so the authorities would abandon her as a hopeless case. (He wondered how much "acting" she might really have to do.)

Now, as he caught his breath on the sofa, Reno absorbed the ambience of the place as Sondra closed the living room drapes and engaged the deadbolt in the door. Her apartment was a shrine to the sixties. Framed posters of Hendrix, Joplin, Morrison, and many of their contemporaries—a goodly number of them no longer around— victims of the success that so often leads to the kind of excess that knocked them out of the game. Some of the posters had ticket stubs tucked inside their frames. Artifacts as genuinely historical as anything you'd find in a museum.

Sondra ducked into a bedroom and reappeared with a lighted stick of incense. Reno got a whiff and said, "Patchouli... you know how to make a guy feel at home."

They talked. About her feelings of apprehension once she'd encouraged him to step forward. About her girlfriend, a fellow abductee, who'd been listening to the radio and called her up. (Sondra, you gotta hear this!) About how she decided to scoop him up if things got out of hand. Then, about the sixties, and do you remember? And sure, I remember—it wasn't that long ago for me. And oh yeah, I forgot. And laughing. In the midst of all, laughing like two stoned out freaks from the days of sex, drugs, and rock 'n' roll.

Then Sondra said, "Take off your clothes."

Reno's mouth fell open, but nothing came out.

"I know, I'm old enough to be your... ah... older sister," she said. "But don't jump to any conclusions. I thought about becoming a nurse once... and anyway, I need to examine you."

"Uh... what for?"

"Implant. Remember, I mentioned that at the meeting? Bet you never thought to do a thorough examination. Anyway, there are some places that would be hard for you to see."

"Now wait a minute. You ain't gonna shine no flashlight up my—"

"Only as a last resort, kiddo. But that's not a common location for tracking devices. They're like us in that respect... who the hell would want to retrieve it? Mine was under the skin on the wrist. It's also likely to find them imbedded inside the nasal cavity. Anyway, strip!"

Reno's cheeks turned rosy. He was not accustomed to feeling bashful around women. He slithered out of his shirt and jeans, leaving his skivvies as the last concession to modesty. He felt chilly. Sondra accommodated him by turning up the heat.

She donned a pair of bifocals and went over him from head to toe, front and back. "You're clean," she announced. "So far, that is. Drop 'em buddy boy."

Reno did as he was told, sitting au naturel before her.

Gingerly, she lifted his penis with two fingers and zeroed in for a closer look.

"BINGO!" she shouted into his crotch. "It's only a few centimeters long..."

"Hey," he said indignantly. I may not be Johnny Wadd, but—"

"I'm talking about the implant, silly. It's on the underside of your wee wee!" In the excitement of her discovery, Sondra absentmindedly tightened her grip on his joystick. She pressed down on the skin with both thumbs in the area where she'd located the device.

It was then she realized that Reno had become a real handful. "Oh MY," she said, gazing down at his member in good standing.

"Oh MY," he said.

"Looks like I've gotten you into another sticky situation."

"Yeah, and you've got to pull me out of it again."

Sondra bowed her head.

"What are you doing?"

"I'm asking forgiveness. My son is about your age." Then she said, "Get ready for the eighth and ninth wonders of the world, kid!" And with that, she lowered her top and freed a pair of the most generous and well preserved fifty year-old breasts in captivity.

"Oh MY!" said Reno for the second time.

"One hundred percent natural... made in America." She leaned over and positioned his banana between her melons. "Come to mama," she said, squeezing them together with her hands.

Seventeen

Tortured, Dan had changed his mind repeatedly during the course of a sleepless night. He showed up at work determined to defend not only his own, but the free speech rights of the entire nation as well.

Twenty minutes before airtime, Sid Kaplan called Dan into his office and shoved the morning paper in his face. Down near the bottom of the front page a smaller headline read: *RENO VEGAS—MISSING AGAIN?*

Dan read on:

KSUK radio personality Dan Rivers, known for trotting out the occasional eccentric or malcontent on his morning talk show, was either the victim of—or as some allege—a willing participant in what appears to be an on-air hoax involving a guest identifying himself as Reno Vegas, one-time local musician who vanished under mysterious circumstances in 1969. The alternative explanation stretches the boundaries of reality as we know it.

Dan tossed the paper aside. "All it means is that people will be listening today. That's the name of the game."

There's more," the GM said, ashen faced. "I received a phone call this morning... All I can say is that some powerful people want this thing killed."

"Or they'll kill us?"

Kaplan, who almost never swore, exploded. "Goddamnit, man... you don't know who you're screwing with!"

Dan saw it clearly now. Apply "gentle" pressure at the one end—that was Milburn's recent visit. Play hardball at the other end—that would be the call from... whom? NASA? CIA? Or Milburn himself, milking it for all it was worth? Whoever it was, they'd spooked Sid Kaplan bigtime.

"I want you to go on the air and state your belief that the person who appeared on your program Monday was a scam artist, which he assuredly is anyway. That's why he's disappeared."

"You didn't see the picture, Sid."

"I'm glad I didn't."

* * *

Cletus Moore checked his calendar. It didn't do any good, because he couldn't remember what day it was yesterday. Nope, you can't tell dog shit about today if you don't remember yesterday. That sounded like some deep philosophical crap. Better to derail that train of thought before it got up a full head of steam. Cletus was a man of simple pleasures. Food, drink... and lately, since a certain exquisite female had been coming around, the joy of giving of oneself.

Yes, it was easy to lose track of time out here in the desert, cut off from the outside world. No TV. Computer? You must be kidding. He did have a radio, though. Radio came from a simpler time, so it wasn't evil—at least not like the technology of today that seemed to be spiraling out of control—manifesting into so many newfangled gadgets and contraptions, all designed to separate you from your money on a continuing basis as you scramble to obtain the latest upgrade. The only thing he listened to on the radio was a little country and western now and then. The rest of it was crap.

Cletus had jumped ship just in the nick of time. Rather than spend the rest of his days in the rat race as a jackass auto mechanic, he'd gotten himself a cabin and a patch of land. When the money ran low, he prayed for help. Then one night it came—straight from the heavens.

The little grey people became his friends.

They were happy to have a remote area to park their craft without being harassed by hysterical humans, or having to run through that take-me-to-your-leader bit, an act they sometimes put on for certain individuals because it was amusing... well, at first anyway. The Greys realized early on that there was no one who could speak for the earthlings, a contentious lot who disagreed and fought over most everything. But Cletus provided them with his unique insight into the human condition, as an artist detached from his creation might assess it in a more objective light. They, in turn, provided him with vittles, booze, and incidentals through their intermediaries—the half human, half alien hybrids living amongst the populace.

The Greys communicated by telepathy, but were also intrigued by the concept of written and spoken language—assigning symbols and sounds to thoughts and arranging them in clever ways. They picked it up rather easily.

Cletus remembered the time a group of them were sitting around his table, drinking. The aliens had developed a taste for the Boones-Farm wine he kept handy. When they got really ripped, they enjoyed telling jokes. The head dude, whose name was Ahmanakananka, but who told Cletus to just call him "Willie," said, "What do you say when you are communicating telepathically and you are suddenly interrupted?"

Everyone looked around the room with eyes as big as plates— because they *were* as big as plates—all except for the earthling, waiting for the punchline.

"Hold that thought!" Willie said.

The room erupted into laughter.

Then Schmeedleborp, one of the taller Greys at around four feet seven, tried his hand at it. "What do you say to a gozeldorf?" he queried.

Again, the anticipatory looks.

"Move, or I will vaporize you!"

Total silence.

Schmeedleborp appeared to be turning red, which is not all that easy for a Grey to do.

"That didn't exactly knock my dick in the dirt," Cletus said.

The Greys looked to one another in bewilderment.

Alter a moment, Willie said, "How delightful, Mister Cletus. Another of your quaint expressions I shall have to commit to my memory banks. Oh... sometime, you must tell me what it means."

Willie had picked up on many of the colloquialisms of the region during his frequent sojourns to the planet--though he sometimes had trouble with idioms. He got so inebriated one night that he puffed out his chest, raised the glass of wine clutched in his three spindly fingers and proclaimed, "I can drink any one of you motherfuckers over the table!" And with that he pitched forward, face down in the bean dip. He had to be portaged back to the ship to sleep it off.

"You wanna hear some poetry? Cletus said.

"Poh-tree?" Willie had that puzzled look again.

"Yeah, here's a good one...listen up."

Cletus's guests strained forward, intent upon capturing every nuance.

Listen, Listen...the cat's a pissin'
Where oh where?
Under the chair
Hurry Mabel, she's under the table
Quick, quick, git the gun
Aw shit, she's done

Cletus sported an adolescent grin as he surveyed each pair of eyes in the room. The aliens appeared to be figuratively scratching their heads.

There was another person besides Cletus who worked as an intermediary for the Greys. It was the woman known as Gretchen. Some time back she'd placed a cryptic two word ad in the newspaper that stated: *Men wanted.* Those who passed the initial screening were given a cover explanation about donating to a sperm bank. Cletus was the only volunteer who actually knew what the "donations" were for.

It was explained to him that Gretchen was the liaison for a group of progressive aliens who considered abductions passe. Why put anyone through the trauma (even these barbarous earthlings) when the fluid of life—that which would beget many human/alien offspring and eventually modify mankind into something more civilized and thus less of a future threat to its celestial neighbors—could be readily extracted from willing participants?

Gretchen had learned—from growing up in earthly society--that with men, it was any excuse to get your rocks off. And so she made the rounds, collecting the precious fluid and storing it away, to be delivered to the Greys at the exchange point, Cletus's cabin.

She was the accommodating type, and when requested, would take the donor organ in hand and help the process along. Employing this method, she found that the rate of repeat donations was virtually one hundred percent. Her attitude was clinical, deriving neither pleasure nor feeling any shame about what she considered to be all in a day's work—the work that was part of something bigger than any individual—indeed, as big as the cosmos.

Cletus knew in his bones that today must be the nineteenth and that soon, beautiful Gretchen would say cheerily, "Time to donate, Cletus... time to do your part." Then, with the situation well in hand—the left one, because that was the arm that had built up the muscle—she'd settle into a nice rhythm that would put him over the top and send him to the moon. (In truth, a part of him WOULD be going to the moon to hook up with a connecting flight to Zeta Reticuli in the constellation Cygnus.) Cletus's affiliation with the aliens was what could be called a mutually satisfying relationship.

That evening, though, as Gretchen got a grip and began working things toward their logical conclusion, she thought of the radio man—Dan Rivers—and felt a twinge of something that could be called "emotion," which was, for the most part, alien to her. She had to admit the feeling was good, in a way, but also confusing, producing an unaccustomed prick of anxiety. And for the first time, she wondered if it were possible that Mister Rivers had not enjoyed the experience of coupling with Brigitta. Surely with men, though, it was any port in a storm—but the possibility that perhaps the deceptive tactics she had used might have caused him some displeasure. Then again, wasn't what she'd arranged along the same lines as a surprise birthday party? Everyone enjoyed those, and Mister Rivers received one JUMBO present.

Gretchen didn't much care for doing the deed, though she'd consented to it a few times just to fit in—for if anyone might feel like an outsider it would surely be someone like her. She wondered if Mister Rivers might put two and two together and be onto who, or what, she was—extrapolating that he'd been the unwilling dupe in a scheme to produce more hybrid offspring.

But he'd be wrong.

These thoughts—the idea that she POSSESSED these thoughts—was disturbing to say the least.

Eighteen

In Tucson, the sunlight seeps into every nook and cranny and imbues the world with a deceptively cheery glow. Stepping from your door, the effusive brightness plays counterpoint to the blues, softening the hard edges of despair, making you doubt the validity of your feelings. But Dan wasn't buying it today as he sat in a dim little piano bar called Ebony and Ivory, ostensibly named after the Stevie Wonder-Paul McCartney anthem to racial harmony.

Yeah, can't we all just get along?

He nursed his whiskey sour and thought about suicide. Not seriously, but at some point, it's an option everyone considers as the shortest distance between two points. What do you do when you've lost your sense of integrity? Being muzzled on the air and coerced into what was essentially a cover up, even if it might be the best thing for all concerned at the moment, was bad enough.

But then there was the matter of the Bitch Goddess Gretchen. Being manipulated like that (in various ways). Humiliation. Rape! There, he said it. And what's more, the possibility that a child may have been conceived on that night—a perverse amalgam of himself and... well, what the hell was she anyway? Human? Alien? An Albanian mud wrestler? It was all too bizarre to consider. And just because, like all men, he had to admit, his brain was ensconced inside his penis. Nonetheless, thoughts of what he might do to the Lady G ran rampant through his mind. How he might return the favor if ever she passed his way again. He could stay up till late at night, occupying every waking moment thinking of creative ways to exact his revenge. Some of them turned him on so much he began to wonder what kind of sick sonofabitch would have such musings.

He forced his mind onto Stacy. Over time, Dan had assumed the role of big brother and confidant, providing a shoulder when one needing crying upon. His co-worker trusted him, and rightly so. Who better to lay man troubles onto than a man—as long as he'll be straight with you—and she knew she could count on Dan for that. So when she put on that long face this morning he figured his misery, and hers, could use some company.

It was just past noon. She was on break and should show any time now. Dum de dum.

The occupants of another table broke into laughter. Dan glanced in their direction and immediately recognized a bunch of obnoxious radio types drinking their lunch. You'd know them anywhere. The gaiety a bit too strained. The behavior a bit too silly. Radio screwballs were always performing.

One of them he knows. It's Brad Gunderson from 103.3. The guy who never removes his tie. Probably sleeps in the damn thing. Makes love to his wife with the tie grazing her tits.

He's in sales now. If you're good at it, that's where the money is. But Dan had no stomach for that game. You've got to be a glad-hander. An A-Number One bullshitter. A sociopath, really, with no qualms about blowing smoke up the ass of any potential client in the effort to convince her that your format is far superior to that of your competitors, even though you're all playing "Bennie And The Jets" every damn day of the week.

Dan watched them huddle and lower their voices. Then Brad got up and moseyed over like some Wild West gunfighter who owns the town.

"Hey Rivers," he said, "That was some ringer you had on your show. Ya know, you'll get into trouble for staging events like that."

"Fuck you, Gunderson."

"Soo… I hear your little outlet is on the block. How much is Fallon offering the old guy?"

SON OF A BITCH! Dan was stunned that the word had gotten out, when there were only three people on the planet that were supposed to know. Stunned, but not surprised. Just another reminder that there were no secrets in this business. One time (at another station in a galaxy far, far away) a listener had called to let him know that he'd be switching shifts with the night guy before Dan had even been informed by management.

A LISTENER! "Nothing's set in stone. They've talked, that's all."

"Yeah, right… have you practiced the phrase: 'You want fries with that?'"

Stacy appeared in the doorway, eyes scanning the darkened room. The sales jerk headed back to friendlier territory, his fat ass flouncing in rhythm to the piano player's rendition of the old Carpenters hit "Close to You."

Dan squeezed off a parting shot. "Better that than to have noose burns around my neck, Gunderson!"

His tormentor flipped him off without looking back.

An hour later, Dan and Stacy were well on their way to becoming shit-faced. Now and then a neck from the rival table would crane in their direction and you knew they were abuzz with speculation as to who the "babe" might be and that they were searching for a plausible excuse to send another envoy over to check it out.

Stacy was a leggy, quietly attractive girl who nonetheless could turn heads in a room, were she to cruise through in a black miniskirt.

Their conversation had been airy and confined to work related matters, but Dan sensed that she was holding back. When her tears gushed he said, "It's Bruno—what's the bastard done to you now?"

Her body convulsed with sobs, she shook her head and tried to speak through salty tears and snot streaming onto her lips. "It... it's not Bruno," she blurted. "He's just a simple, overly jealous dope who can't control his emotions."

"Then who is it?"

"It's Fallon, Dan... it's MIKE FALLON. He asked me to lunch last Friday. To be polite I accepted, knowing he was someone important, hanging with the old man and all that. He told me about his big plans to buy the station. Then he drops the bomb. Wants to keep me on as his personal assistant. He's going to DOUBLE my salary just for starters. Says he might need me to travel with him sometimes—going first class, of course, staying in the best hotels and everything."

Dan had found it curious that following his meetings with Sid Kaplan, Fallon had not immediately left town to tend to his other holdings. He'd seen the man subsequently pop in and out of the station a few times, but gave it no further thought. Now, the clouds were lifting.

"I may be young but I'm not dumb," she continued. "The way he looks at me, I know what he's going to be expecting sooner or later..."

"Wait a MINUTE, girl—you're not staying on with that scumbag. He's got a wife and two young boys."

"I can't afford to lose my job now. I've got credit card debt. School loans to pay off. Please don't say anything to him, Dan. This could be my big opportunity. Promise me, now. I mean, you've always told me you've got to weigh the good against the bad, and nothing's perfect... is it?"

It came flooding back to him now. That night he and Maya had the fight. What was it about? Strange, now, that something could set off a life altering chain reaction in two people's lives and the seed of it gets buried under the rubble of time. Like the screak of a solitary bird reverberating through the walls of a desert canyon, the consequences of our actions regenerate and feed-off themselves.

The argument had occurred over the phone. They left it alone for a couple hours, then Maya called and said I don't like feeling this way and so they had pretty much made up and agreed to rendezvous at this hippie joint where they sometimes hung out. They were to meet at eight. Dan planned to be late—accidentally on purpose. He was still smarting from things that had been said and to make her wait would create a certain amount of anxiety, he figured, and that would put him one up on her.

Maya waited till eight-thirty. Dan had never been more than ten minutes late since she'd known him. Anxiousness turned to anger and she stormed out to the parking lot.

Her car wouldn't start.

Nothing but silence, save for the muted cacklings of some drunks behind the building and the sound of piss raining on dirt. She went back into the bar—saw no familiar faces. Nothing to do but sit for a minute and assess the situation. She looked at her watch. Dan wasn't going to show.

A young patron approached and engaged her in conversation. He had shoulder length hair and a beard--a freak, like her--so she did not feel uncomfortable. (In subsequent years, when even country music stars converted from flat-tops to flowing locks, all bets would be off).

After he'd coaxed the story out of her, he alluded to the obvious— that there wouldn't be any mechanics around to look at the car tonight. Let it sit and call the shop in the morning. He'd be happy to give her a lift home, he said with a disarming smile. If she TRUSTED him, of course.

And maybe—just maybe—with a single act of betrayal to one's own kind, this was where it all started to unravel.

The end of the innocence.

Sometime after midnight they found her. She had managed to stagger into a neighbor's yard, bloodied and busted up. Raped and beaten to within an inch of her life. Maya spent weeks in the hospital and needed corrective surgery on her face. The doctors did their best, but she would never again look exactly like the pretty young girl Dan had met on the beach.

During his daily visits to her bedside, Dan determined that he had missed her by about a minute.

Sixty seconds.

The truth—oh God—he couldn't lay the truth of why he'd been late onto her. Not now, at least. So he said that he'd had car trouble as well. What a weird configuration of planets there must have been to cause both of their vehicles to crap out on the same night.

Maya recovered physically, but something had died in her. Dan tried to keep the relationship together, but she became increasingly withdrawn. One day she told him that she needed time to be alone. She moved back to Iowa to live with her parents. He wrote. She wrote back. For a while. Then her letters stopped.

They never caught the guy that did it.

And that was what Dan had had to live with during the balance of his long strange trip. And it was why, as he sat there looking at Stacy, no longer hearing her words, he saw the face of innocence doomed.

Nineteen

Gretchen considered herself fortunate. Fortunate to have inherited the best physical traits of her human/alien parentage. High, firm breasts. Perfectly tapered legs. Exotic Nancy Kwan looks that would put movie stars to shame. But the eyes were what really stood out. They were large, as one might expect—not to the point where anyone might suspect an otherworldly lineage—but certainly to the degree that people found them remarkable.

She was fortunate also to be doing such important work. To be a soldier in service of the greater good of the cosmos, and there could be no doubt that the ever expanding effort to engineer a new race of beings—genes infused with eons of knowledge and experience from both cultures—was the most significant undertaking in their respective histories.

She never knew her father. Ironically, he had been one of those anonymous human donors, like the men she "collected" from on a regular basis. And though she'd met her mother, Aieena, whom Gretchen assumed was still out there on an interplanetary mission somewhere, the two of them were essentially strangers as well.

She'd been raised by her adoptive Chinese-American parents. Growing up, she devoured all of the Superman comics she could get her hands on. Peculiar, perhaps, for a girl, but within those pages she developed an instant rapport with a character that had also arrived from another world to be brought up by an earthly couple. Thinking about those days only served to underscore her lamentable lack of affinity with most of the "purebreds."

Her thoughts turned again to Mister Dan Rivers. She found he was entering her mind more frequently as of late. And again she wondered if he'd enjoyed the experience of coupling with her friend Brigitta. No, Gretchen didn't take to too many people, but when she did, a fierce loyalty would develop, and she would do most anything for the person. Her affiliation with Brigitta was, at least outwardly, a marriage of beauty and beast rarely seen among homo sapiens, who, in their shallow way, tended to gravitate toward those of their own financial, intellectual, or corporeal station.

She had seen the looks of despair upon Brigitta's face when men would stare at her with a mixture of revulsion and curiosity. And maybe it was spurred on by her own metamorphosis—this thing that was taking place inside her brain—because she knew that her human friend was sad. And so she devised a plan, thinking only of providing joy, or at the very least, a rollicking good time, for someone she cared about. There was never any consideration for the feelings of the designated "stud." After all, her other friend Alice had remarked that HER boyfriend would stick his dick in a hole in the ground if he thought a snake might lick it.

So where were these curious stirrings—this giddiness whenever she thought about Mister Dan Rivers—coming from? And why the sudden concern for HIS feelings? She wanted to call him. No, better not. Anyway, if she did, the only number she had was the direct line into the KSUK control room—the line Dan used to put callers on the air.

Would she dare?

Twenty-four hours later, Gretchen had decided not to call. Definitely not. He would misinterpret her intentions. If only she knew what her intentions were. All the more reason to avoid it. Living in a state of confusion was, well... uncomfortable. And Mister Dan Rivers seemed to be the source of that confusion.

She peered out the window. Quiet neighborhood. Lots of shade trees. Residents who turned in before the Tonight Show started. In another week she'd be moving to the next location. New place, same routine.

Water the plants. Collect the mail and bring in the newspapers. It was best this way—that no one got to know her too well.

She took a stack of newspapers from the dining room table, sat down, and placed them in her lap. She skimmed through them, looking mainly at the headlines. Nothing of much interest. She yawned. Thought she might turn in. Making the papers neat again, she almost missed it. But there it was, down near the bottom on the front page: *RENO VEGAS MISSING AGAIN?* And below that the name: Dan Rivers.

She sped through the story. My god, a terrible mistake had been made. The Greys she knew would not intentionally do something like this. Abductions and invasive physical examinations had occurred in the past, but they weren't into totally disrupting people's lives.

She went out to the back patio—into the cool night air. With no moon, the stars had the stage to themselves. Fate had stepped in. It looked like she would be contacting a certain party after all.

Twenty

Agent Lawrence Milburn sat at his desk, thinking things through. Reno Vegas, and he knew in his gut that it WAS the real Reno, had vanished for the second time. This time, though, Milburn was pretty sure the kid was still on terra firma. The key, he figured, was the radio guy. Dan Rivers wasn't the sort who would drop Vegas like a hot potato—even though he had played the whole thing down on subsequent shows, stating in retrospect that he didn't get a good enough look at the photo to make any determination—and what were the chances of a cockamamie story like that being true in the first place?

No, he wouldn't drop it. Somewhere, somehow, Rivers would make contact. Keep tabs on the radio guy and he'll lead you to your quarry. Then you nab Vegas and shut him up. Take him out of circulation. Make him disappear for the third and final time.

Good thing the wire services hadn't picked it up. As long as the story stayed contained, as long as no one really believed in its validity, Milburn would be free to conduct his own unofficial investigation.

With the grace of God, his "condition" wouldn't significantly interfere. They called it narcolepsy. Sudden onset of brief, but deep sleep. You never knew when it was going to strike. Should his superiors in the Bureau get wind of it, his career could be in jeopardy. It would be a fine line he'd have to walk to save the world from chaos without drawing undue attention to himself, but it would be worth it.

He glanced over at Geraldine. She was looking a little parched, so he dribbled some water onto her. Geraldine was the geranium whose job was to sit in her pot and soak up sun at her post near the window.

She was his friend and confidante--the only one if you got right down to it.

He could talk to her and she never gave him any shit.

He gave her diminutive red petals a little pat as he left the room.

* * *

Sondra applied the finishing touches to Reno's cheeks. A bit of blush for a rosy, healthy looking complexion. She'd already applied the foundation and mascara (Reno's eyelashes were long, so there was no need for "falsies"), and the look was almost complete.

"Let's get this wig on you," she said, "then you can look in the mirror."

"Jesus," he said, "I never thought I'd end up a transvestite."

"Aw, c'mon—didn't you ever fantasize about wearing your mother's clothes when you were little?"

"I imagined my mother WITHOUT her clothes..."

"Figures." Sondra set the wig into place and said, "You're about to find out why blondes have more fun."

Reno appraised himself in the bedroom dresser mirror. "Damn!" he said. "I'm one gorgeous chick."

"I remember that line from *Midnight Cowboy*, I think. Now practice the voice."

"The rain in Spain falls mainly on the-"

"Not like that! You sound like Frankie Valli on "Walk Like a Man.""

"But sing like a woman."

"Maybe a whiskey voice is the way to go. Lots of sexy women have them."

"How long will I have to be female?"

"Until we can find a way for you to hitch a ride back to where you came from."

* * *

"Line two, you're on the air."

"Guess you're pretty busy... the line's been tied up this morning."

That voice. Something familiar about it. "Hey, it shows people like you are listening."

"Guess you're always tied up—one way or the other... MISTER Rivers."

Goddamn... it was HER! "Uh, yeah... well... listen, you're the thirty-seventh caller this morning and that means you've won a prize! Hold on the line while we do this break." Dan punched up a spot, removed his headphones and grabbed the receiver.

"Gretchen, listen... I— I want to talk to you."

"You ARE talking to me Mister Ri—"

"I mean, uh, I want to see you... but not at your place."

"Are you mad at me?"

Keep calm. Keep cool. Don't betray a hint of anger or you'll lose her. "No... I was just... disappointed the three of us didn't get to share a cigarette afterwards."

"Okay, I know a place."

* * *

Dan peered warily into the back seat. He wasn't taking any chances that Brigitta might be lurking, ready to pounce upon him again. He felt apprehensive about being a passenger in Gretchen's car, and he wondered if he was crazy or just plain stupid to allow her to take control of the situation, to put his life (if not his privates) in her hands again—and it was only the tone of her voice over the phone that made him want to believe that this time she was sincere. And anyway, he was the trusting sort—or it seemed he was becoming so, perhaps something he'd absorbed from Maya—a tendency to want to believe in the innate goodness of people, despite the occasional rotten apple.

He installed himself in the passenger seat of her Jetta.

"Hi," she said.

"Hi," he said.

Silence. Then both of them trying to speak at the same time.

"After you," he said.

"No, after you," she said.

"You've got a lot of explaining to do. Number one: ARE you, or have you ever been an alien, or an E.T., or one of those out of this world whatchamacallits?" Listening to himself, he couldn't believe what he was saying. "Number two: Were you using me to impregnate that hippo accomplice of yours to produce some half human--half alien god knows what type of offspring? You need to come clean with me here if you expect to gain my trust from this point forward."

"Are you quite finished, Mister Rivers...or is there more?"

"That will do for a start."

She put the key in the ignition. He told her to wait, astonishing himself. Where did he get the balls to tell HER what to do—for all he knew she might shoot some laser beam out of her eyes and paralyze him—or worse. But righteous indignation makes a man fearless.

"The answers are yes... and no," she said, staring straight ahead.

"Jesus, are we playing twenty questions?"

"Yes, I AM out of this world, as you put it... I'm also OF this world, and it's not something I reveal to anyone who isn't totally trustworthy, as I know you will be, due to my finely tuned intuition for such things."

"Well, I have a finely tuned B.S. meter... just so you know."

"Anyway, the ace I hold is that virtually no one would believe you even if you did try to expose me."

She told him the whole story, ending with, "The possibility that you may not have been totally pleased with our date has only recently entered my mind."

It was good to know that Brigitta was just your garden-variety earthling... he supposed. But her stunning partner in crime wasn't about to get off that easy. "What you did was called bait and switch, baby. False advertising."

And because he still felt like the somebody who was wronged in that "Another Somebody Done Somebody Wrong Song," he wasn't really listening—not close enough anyway—to cull his epiphany not from what was being said, but from the way she said it. And so he blustered on, making his case like a good district attorney.

Then he stopped. He reflected on something she'd said moments ago: *I am rather singular of purpose, Mister Rivers.* Had that really come out of her mouth? While he was boiling, she was as cool as Houdini in handcuffs. Cool and... CALCULATING. That was it! Jesus, what had he expected? This was part of her makeup—as one of THEM. She was like a cat sitting on your chest, purring away as he digs his claws into you—having a high old time, oblivious to your pain.

And in that moment, something shifted in his mind.

She went on to the other purpose she had for seeing him—the Reno Vegas affair. Would he be able to re-establish contact with the young man? If so, she would set up a meeting with her associate, Cletus--a precursor, hopefully, to a close encounter with the Greys. If anybody could rectify the mistake that had displaced that poor man in time, they were the ones. "I want you to be along for this meeting," she said, "because I feel it only proper that I make things right with you... and I want to show you what is real."

Twenty-One

Dan sat in his office. Two days had passed since he'd cleared the air with Gretchen. He felt good about that, but this Reno Vegas business had him stumped. The guy hadn't left a forwarding address as he dashed out the back door of the station with that gaggle of goons in hot pursuit. Unless Reno saw fit to contact him, Dan didn't know what he could do.

Then the phone rang.

* * *

"We have to go," Sondra said.

"Where?"

"While I was out, I called Dan Rivers at the radio station. I wanted to see how hot you were... are. He says you're hot all right, but locally—he's heard nothing of it on the networks. There's this local fed, though, name of Milburn you've got to steer clear of. Rivers thinks we should try to get you out of the area." Facing the bedroom closet, she spoke with her back toward him. She was trying to decide which tube top to wear. "We have to meet with Rivers." She turned to face Reno. "He's spoken with someone who may be able to get you back."

* * *

Sondra kept the Camaro within the speed limit.

Reno adjusted his wig. "Where are we meeting them?" he asked.

"Tucson Mall. Lots of bodies to blend in with."

Reno felt uncomfortable with words like "bodies."

"We'll be switching vehicles and riding with Rivers and his friend on the chance that you and I are being tailed," she continued. "After that, you know as much as I do."

Reno needed to make a pit stop. Sondra said okay, we'll pull into that Denny's over there—but make it quick. He entered the restaurant wearing blue jeans and sneakers. Shaving his legs was not a concession to femininity he cared to make—but his "hair" was perfectly coiffed, makeup expertly applied, and as Sondra put it, he was a knockout.

He made his way down the hallway to those doors with the universal man-woman symbols—the female icon still sporting a dress here in the modern era of jumbled sexuality. Instinctively, he placed his hand on the men's door, caught himself, took a deep breath, and gently shouldered his way through the opposite portal.

Relieved to find that the ladies room was empty, Reno selected a stall and latched the door. Oh man, he thought—if I'm gonna do this right, I've got to squat to pee. Better go with the flow, so to speak, and play this thing to the hilt in case anyone comes in.

As he took care of business, two young women entered the room just to gaze at themselves in the mirror—jabbering excitedly in the way that those imbued with more glamour than gray matter are wont to do.

1st chick: "I just HATE Lupita, know what I mean?"

2nd chick: "Yeah, I know what ya mean."

1st chick: "She's always talking behind people's backs."

2nd chick: "Turn your back, she'll talk about you."

1st chick: "She's a bitch, man."

2nd chick: "She's a whore, man."

1st chick: "She's a big fucking slut."

2nd chick: "You going to her party Friday night?"

1st chick: "Yeah, I'm going."

2nd chick: "Me too—let's go together."

1st chick: "Cool... it's gonna be so much fun!!"

Reno heard the door swing open as the girls scurried out of the room, tittering excitedly as their voices faded down the hall.

Back in the car, Sondra said, "How'd it go?"

"Uh... little by little I'm gaining more insight into the female condition."

* * *

They gathered round the large circle where the desert vegetation had been flattened. The others—Reno, Sondra, Gretchen, and Cletus—seemed to regard the "landing pad" with reverence. This almost proves it, Dan thought.

He had a feeling that Cletus regarded him with some trepidation. The big bear of a man had been cordial enough, in a gruff sort of way, but the eyes don't lie. They had all had their close encounters. They were "experienced," as Jimi Hendrix would put it. He was an outsider.

Dan also sensed, in Cletus's deference to the exotic beauty, that Gretchen was in charge.

She looked at Cletus. "When will they be returning?"

The bewhiskered one dug his fingers a little deeper inside his dirt encrusted overalls and played pocket pool. It was a conditioned reflex, as he became automatically aroused whenever Gretchen was around. Unfortunately, she would not be "collecting" today. "Around Christmas time," he replied.

She frowned.

Anticipating her next question, Cletus said, "I don't have no cell phone number for the ship or nothing like that."

Gretchen, who had earlier taken Reno aside for about fifteen minutes, turned to him and said, "I have no reason to doubt you, Mister Vegas. I know the Greys. They will take you back. But you will have to keep a low profile until then. In conversing with Mister Rivers, it appears the future would be precarious for you in this present time reality."

Clouds hung low on the horizon, glowing with fire. A soft evening breeze toyed with Gretchen's dark tresses. Her eyes made a sweep of the group. "I will be in touch with Cletus," she said. At that, the big guy's hands dug deeper still into his pockets. "When the time comes, Mister Vegas, you will hear from me. And now, we should be getting back."

As Gretchen's Jetta pulled slowly back onto the road, a lone figure lay pressed against the earth, amongst the cholla and prickly pear, on a ridge overlooking Cletus's cabin. Maverick FBI agent Lawrence

Milburn trained his binoculars on the vehicle. "THREE OF 'EM," he muttered. Three hot looking bitches—one raven-haired, one redhead, one blonde. That Rivers was probably porking all three of them. RADIO PERVERTS!

And who was that Grizzly Adams guy who appeared to be fingering something inside his bib overalls? A weapon? Whatever was going on, the agent was convinced that Dan Rivers held the key to the whereabouts of Reno Vegas, and he'd be on him like stink on shit until Rivers tipped his hand.

Rising to his feet, Milburn momentarily lost his balance. He backed into the nearest prickly pear and became acutely aware that Reno Vegas wasn't going to be his only pain in the ass.

Twenty-Two

Dan felt surprisingly upbeat, considering that he'd soon—in all likelihood—be out of a job, his actions were under scrutiny by the authorities, and he was dating a space alien. Qualify that—she was half human, and that was about all you could say for half the people he knew.

It hadn't been your normal type of beginning. On their first date, Dan had sex—Gretchen didn't. Where you go from there is anybody's guess. And strange as it would have seemed on the morning after that found him with murder in his eyes, he was now looking forward to their next encounter.

There was so much to learn about her—so many questions. In a way, he still felt like this was a fantasy—that the lot of them could very well be mentally unstable and this whole flying saucer business no more than a delusion they shared. But to be a total skeptic, here and now, with all that had passed before his eyes—a beloved president and a civil rights leader gunned down, Watergate, Vietnam, hanky-panky in the Oval Office—one would have to be delusional to blindly accept the official version of things. Half truths. Manipulation of public opinion through the media. Outright lies. A bit of the conspiracy theorist must exist in all who have traveled this road, and thus a mind that is open to thinking the unthinkable.

* * *

"I want to know all about you," he said. "But only what you feel comfortable in revealing."

They had a window table at the Blue Peacock Café on Fourth Avenue. Out on the street, the turn of the millennium hippies strolled by. They had the *look* down at least.

A grandfatherly type sitting at a table across the room from them hadn't taken his eye off Gretchen since the couple arrived. Unfazed, he spooned soup into his nose.

Dan lowered his voice. "For example, do you have any special powers that we regular run-of-the-mill earth denizens don't possess?" He felt like a ten-year-old interviewing Clark Kent.

"You've already seen it," she replied.

He gave her a quizzical look.

"I have the ability to turn men on sexually."

"This is news?"

"As soon as they look into my eyes."

They walked down Fourth Avenue, peering into the windows of used clothing boutiques, a used record store, the funky bars populated by those who've been used and abused.

Dan's mind was churning. He'd held off on the follow-up question as long as he could. "So that's how you made me respond to your friend, Jabba the Hutt?"

"That isn't charitable, Mister Rivers. She's a little overweight, I'll admit... but she has a good heart."

A young loiterer eyed them. He wore a brown leather jacket over layers of clothes, and heavy engineer boots—too warm for the early November eighty-degree daytime weather, but the homeless are not habituated to frequent costume changes.

"Dude, can I have five bucks for some pizza?"

Dan waved him off. "Sorry, man," he said. (Whatever happened to a quarter for the bus, which used to be the panhandling standard? Inflation, he supposed. Anyway, give to one and you have to give to all—and that could result in a feeding frenzy.)

Farther on, it became a gauntlet. Clusters of them. Street kids. Street dogs.

Gretchen stopped to communicate with an Akita attached to a blonde-haired waif. "Has he eaten today?" she asked the girl.

"Yeah," the blonde responded. "We do okay. We go around to the cafes at closing time. They're usually pretty good to us... there's always something."

The dog sniffed Gretchen's fingers. She knelt and allowed the animal to nudge her face and apply some slurpy tongue action to her cheeks.

Dan was broadsided by a wave of emotion—the sudden realization of how beautiful this remarkable woman was becoming in both body and spirit.

"How long have you been out here?" she asked the girl.

"A few weeks. But I'm getting off the streets, man. Getting it together. Going to settle down and do something practical with my life." She produced a cigarette from her backpack and fumbled around for a match. "Yeah... I'm gonna race sled dogs in Alaska."

On their next date, they rented a movie and watched it at Dan's place. *Plan 9 From Outer Space* carried the reputation of being the worst film ever made. Gretchen laughed at the hokey costumes and inept special effects. They hugged goodnight and shared their first serious kiss.

They devoted a full day to exploring the musty corridors of used bookstores. Dan picked up an anthology of true crime stories as investigated by the FBI. Gretchen came away with a pristine copy of *Men Are From Mars, Women Are From Venus.*

They checked out a poetry reading downtown. A woman from out of state had just published a chapbook with one of the local presses. She stood in front of the thirty or so attendees and read several of her poems, which were filled with disjointed images—sentence fragments that picked up and left off in the middle of nowhere. The poet sounded bored. A white-haired gentleman in the second row nodded off. Gretchen placed her hand on Dan's knee.

Her current digs—another luxury home in the Catalina foothills— afforded Gretchen a courtyard with an intricate maze. She stood at the entrance and said, "You'll find me in the middle... if you find me. Wait five minutes and then go for it!" Then she was gone.

Dan sighed. He understood that she was being playful, but anything that smacked of possible deception was still a sore point with him. A vision of Brigitta, naked and sweaty, flashed through his mind. Shit. If she were waiting in there, they'd have a hell of a fight on their hands trying to pin him down to do the dirty deed this time. But a modicum of trust was being established here; and so he estimated the time and plunged into the labyrinth of tall green hedges.

An aerial shot from the Goodyear blimp would have shown a figure in erratic motion, pinballing in one direction and then the next—with great fervor initially, then a more plodding, deliberate determination—and finally, a throwing up of the hands in desperation. Dan was almost ready to call out to her, but that would be admitting defeat, and he would not allow her to get the best of him again.

He stood quietly, finally grasping that he needed to give it up to the universe and wait for divine inspiration. A little voice told him to turn right at the next opening and to simply keep going.

Suddenly, the world opened up again and he stood at the edge of the clearing. And in the middle, on a white stone bench, sat Gretchen. Naked. All except for a pair of black stiletto heels.

She stood and said, "It's about time, Mister Rivers."

She was a study in contrasts—the shiny black mane and the dark silky patch between her thighs juxtaposed strikingly against her ivory skin. Her breasts were firm and high, with cylindrical nipples jutting like miniature doorknobs, inviting his fingers to give them a twist. Her shapely legs were made even sexier looking by her choice of footwear. "It's taken a while," she said, "but I'd like to atone for past transgressions."

He stood there, unable to move or speak, dumbstruck by the dazzling totality of her.

She walked up to him, unzipped his pants, and removed his boner. She stroked it a few times, then leaned into him and rubbed the head along the moist furrow of her secret garden.

He tried to speak but it sounded like infant babble.

She punched him hard in the shoulder. Then in a voice one would use to explain things to a child, she said, "Mister Rivers…you may have your way with me now.”

Their lovemaking was tender and sweet. She was like a pump that needed to be primed. The first few strokes produce no response. This was her trust issue. But over the next few nights—sometimes at her place, sometimes at his—Dan settled into a serious groove, intimating in every possible way that he was no fly-by-night fucker— no way, mama—no games. Just me giving you the best boning you've ever had—or die trying--you fine transmundane mama. And so, gradually, she began to gush with the kinds of sounds he wanted to hear—reaching her climaxes half moaning, half cooing into his ear—half again as sweet as anything he'd ever heard.

Twenty-Three

Driving home from work, Dan stopped for the light and pulled up alongside a young stud blasting the stereo in his jacked up SUV with the obligatory oversize tires. The kid's windows were rolled up and all one could hear was the dull repetitive thumping of the bass, loud enough to rattle the windows of nearby shops. Where the hell did a snotnose barely old enough to shave, sporting an ass-backwards baseball cap, obtain the funds to be cruising in the likes of such a mean machine when Dan and his old beater were getting ready to celebrate their tenth anniversary together?

He wasn't going to let it bother him—the kid would be deaf by the time he entered prison.

He boosted the volume on KSUK. It was three days before Thanksgiving and the two network sports weirdos, Robert and Bob, were still yammering about baseball—the odious Yankees of all things. How many fans in Tucson could give a crap about the Yankees? Ah, the beauty of one-size-fits-all satellite radio. Dan wasn't going to let that get to him either.

Not today.

He went home and made a big bowl of popcorn, called Harvey onto his lap and fed the dog as much as he wanted. He pulled a package of cookies from the cupboard and tried to open it with his bare hands, the way you used to be able to open things, but which now—in the age of adult-proof packaging—was an impossibility. No problem. He fished a pair of wire cutters from the tool drawer.

Two is a couple, three would be a few... and more than three would qualify as several. Okay—he'd had sex with Gretchen on SEVERAL occasions! That almost made them a couple, didn't it? Hmmm... where was this line of thinking going to lead? He didn't want to project any further—that would be presumptuous.

The thought of what their kids might look like popped into his head.

Man, that was dumb. Need to keep reminding yourself that even though she looks human, there's another species involved here. You know, like a horse and a donkey—they produce a mule. Well, can you even tell the difference between a mule and a donkey, Mister Smart Guy? Soooo... maybe it could work out after all.

Silly rabbit, to be thinking such things at all.

Anyway, he felt happy. For the first time in a while. And he'd be seeing her again tonight. But feeling happy apparently took something out of you. He crawled onto the bed. Harv was already there, lying on his side and looking bloated from an overdose of popcorn. A nap would do them both good.

They were out in less than sixty seconds.

He woke with a start. The phone was ringing. He tumbled out of bed and tripped over shoes, clothes, and chew toys scattered about the floor. Goddamnit! But he made it to the phone in time.

It was her.

She called him "Mister Rivers." In the beginning she had done this out of a sense of propriety. Now, she was being playful. He still didn't much care for it.

"I'm so sorry," she began. "I have to cancel our date tonight."

And there it was... that familiar sinking feeling.

"Remember, I told you about my volunteer work in the community?"

"You touched on it... briefly."

"I'd forgotten that I have an appointment tonight to collect a ... donation."

He was disappointed. First with her—then with himself for being disappointed. He knew it was too early in the game to be thrown off stride by one little curveball... but there it was. And what kind of volunteer work could this be on a Saturday night? What kind of work, indeed...

Stake out.

He knew it wasn't right, but there he sat in his car a block down the street from her place. He'd cruised by to see if the lights were on, then took up his position to wait. He only hoped that when Gretchen left she wouldn't turn in his direction and bust him on the spot.

He glanced at the digital display on his dashboard clock.

Twenty minutes later a pair of headlights moved slowly away from the house, hesitated momentarily at the end of the driveway, then turned onto the roadway as her Jetta sped off in the opposite direction, heading west.

He followed at a discreet distance.

She led him to a residence on the burgeoning northwest side, a part of town growing so fast—eating further into the desert with each passing day—Dan hardly recognized it.

When he was certain she'd entered the house, he killed the motor and crept to the front porch, pressing simultaneously on the heel and ball of each foot—the flat step the Indians had used (he'd read somewhere) to become silent and deadly.

The drapes were closed, but a sliver of an opening remained, just large enough for him to peer into the living room with his eye pressed right to the window.

He didn't want to believe it.

Furious, he tried the door. The knob twisted in his hand. AHA! They had been careless. But he would be cool, or at least project the outward appearance of calm. He opened the door and stepped inside, expecting the two of them to run for cover. They didn't.

"Dan!" she cried, calling him by his given name for the first time. "What on earth do you think you're doing?"

He didn't have a ready-made answer—but he could see what SHE was doing. And what was incredulous was that she wasn't stopping. He figured the guy would've jumped up and tried to whack him by now, but he was an old buzzard—sitting there as if he were getting a haircut, eyes turning glassy and tongue lolling out of his mouth—the only whacks being administered by the woman Dan had been dating.

"You just can't burst in here and interfere with my work," she said sternly, as she continued to "work" the old dude's root in rhythmic fashion.

My God, he thought, she's a call girl—and an unrepentant one at that. His knees felt weak and he thought he might lose his balance.

"Get a grip on yourself!" she said.

This was an outrage. "For Chrissake, don't you even have enough shame to stop?"

"I can't," she shouted, nodding toward the subject in hand. "HE'S ABOUT TO EJACULATE!!"

Twenty-Four

Dan switched the radio to the "Morning Zoo" on 103.3, the station Brad Gunderson worked for. Nearly every FM outlet up and down the dial had a similar show—two inane dudes who think they're funnier than they are, and a news chick doubling as the obligatory live laugh track for the jokes delivered by Tim and Tom, Bob and Rob, or whoever the tedious, interchangeable hosts might be.

Dan's life was becoming a zoo. He tried to think of some way to give Gretchen the benefit of the doubt, but he couldn't shake the image of her milking that old bastard—the contented cow expression on his face—and she looking so innocent like a kid pumping self-serve ice cream into a cup. How could he be serious about someone whose hand would always be down someone else's pants?

He spent Thanksgiving alone.

Gretchen sunned herself on the patio of her borrowed digs. How could she reason with someone so pig headed? She'd tried to explain to him the importance of the "program," and that it was neither here nor there but just simple reality—there being no monetary funds to compensate the donors—that most of them would not be inclined to participate in the absence of her helping hands approach.

But emotions—and this was something she was trying to come to grips with herself, and thus could understand on at least a rudimentary level—had obviously gotten the best of Mister Rivers.

Would he ever come around and listen to reason? He would need to, because there could be no compromise on this issue.

That evening, when shadows fell and the natural world grew silent, she imagined the slumbering estate revived by the drone of familiar voices. The clatter of dishes--the rattle of pots and pans. It was an eerie quiet. Like someone had pressed the pause button and everything went into suspended animation.

Waiting.

Homes feel homeless in the absence of the ones they love.

She spent Thanksgiving alone.

On the day after, Dan went to the mall. It would be the biggest shopping day of the year. The joint would be mobbed with bargain hunters. He felt starved for human contact, even though he'd essentially be alone in a sea of strangers. They'd be festive strangers, though, and the place would be decked out in holiday finery.

He ducked into a couple of the larger department stores, just to see if he might soak up some of the glow from the artificial greenery bedecked in a myriad of twinkling colored lights. Farther down the main corridor, Santa was holding court for all little munchkins who, unawares, were fueling the economy with dreams of plastic stuff dancing in their heads—stuff that would soon be making a brief layover at Jennifer's, and Mario's, and Ashley's house on its inexorable journey to the landfill.

A woman with ash blonde hair curled in tiny ringlets entered his field of vision for a moment and disappeared again into the crowd. He worked his way through the swarm of bodies (one could easily imagine himself on a city street in China) and fell in step behind her.

From the back, she looked like Maya.

He tried to be inconspicuous, as on that day long ago when he'd first noticed her on the beach. When the woman stopped to peer into a shop window, he pretended to be checking out one of the places she'd already passed.

Of course, it wasn't Maya. Couldn't be. Then again, there was always a one in three hundred million chance that it COULD be her, come to the desert to look for him.

She entered a women's clothing boutique. He figured he'd loiter around outside until she emerged. He became impatient and went inside. Hip-hop music boomed from invisible speakers. A young salesgirl intercepted him and did the how-can-I-help-you routine. He felt embarrassed. He told her he'd just look around a bit. His quarry was thumbing through a rack of blouses. He still could not see her face. The salesgirl hovered, throwing surreptitious glances his way. Did she think it odd that a middle-aged man would be shopping for his wife in a place that caters to twenty-somethings?

And then it hit him.

This YOUNG woman he'd been tailing could not be Maya. She'd be close to his age now. He had slipped into a fantasy world. He felt tears welling up and headed blindly for the exit.

At that moment, he knew there was someone he needed to see.

Twenty-Five

"There's still a lot of stuff I don't get," Reno said. "Like the war. I understand that now we're on friendly terms with the same bunch we were fighting back then."

He gazed up at the night sky—a black shroud speckled with pinpricks of light. "It was called the domino theory... remember?"

"Of course," said Dan.

"That's how they justified it, man. The red menace would take over the world if we didn't stop it then and there. Well, we lost—and now they say communism is DEAD? That's creepy, man."

Dan took a long pull from his beer. The desert was cooling fast and he thought about retrieving his jacket from the tent. The camping trip had been his idea. Being mirror images of one another (Reno would be about Dan's same age had things taken their normal course), he sensed that the two of them needed to get to the nub of something— to arrive somewhere together and examine what they found.

And so he began. "On the deepest level, it seems to be a basic human need to band together in tribes and manufacture some excuse to raise hell with some other tribe. Decades later, in retrospect, the reasons don't make any sense... but then we turn around and do the same stupid stuff all over again. And since full-fledged wars have been hard to come by lately, we've got that little thing we call the War on Drugs."

Reno got to his feet and paced around the campfire. "That's one thing I never would have believed if someone had told me back then." His face partially-illuminated by the flames, the girlish image the fugitive time traveler projected was even more alluring than normal—and more ironic to Dan, considering his own romantic foibles of late. But they both knew that, with what was at stake, it would be prudent to remain Roberta, rather than Reno--even out her in the middle of nowhere.

"It isn't really about drugs, Reno. That's just a symbol. It's about altered states of consciousness. If there's any legitimate knock against our generation, it's that we took the easy path to get there when we could and should have delved more into the natural highs—yoga, meditation—that sort of thing. Same end result but without the nasty side effects. But we all possessed a kind of innocence about it, and because of that, there were excesses. We were pioneers in space exploration, if you will—and we did all the succeeding generations a favor by showing them what can happen when you carry a good thing too far. Today, unfortunately, some have chosen to ignore those lessons.

"Anyway, 'Make Love Not War' was a threat to all the vested interests who get rich on making war, or at least keeping us prepared for war, often referred to as the military-industrial complex—a term we heard bandied about more often in your day than now. The powers that be saw that certain drugs--cannabis and the psychedelics especially—had a tendency to make people less aggressive. Maybe they envisioned a time when the majority of Americans would be pacifists, and, of course, that wouldn't do. Who was going to go out and fight their wars? But I think most intelligent people can see that what it's turned into—drug lords knocking each other and innocent bystanders off as well... swat teams knocking down people's doors... forfeiture of property without a conviction... filling the prisons up with nonviolent offenders... has moved us a little farther down the road toward a police state.

"Just like a real war, though, it's good for the economy. Keeps a whole shitload of cops, judges, corrections officers, parole and probation officers, administrative personnel, ad agencies that produce anti-drug radio and TV spots, and a host of others who are in on the action working."

"Whoa, man. Shit!" Reno made a show of walking around behind Dan to touch his back.

"What're you doing?"

"Looking for the key that wound you up, Mister radio dude." Dan drained his beer, and as he did, his head tilted skyward. Switching gears, he said, "Every radio show that's ever been broadcast is hurtling through the void as we speak."

"That IS far out."

"Traveling to God knows where. ONLY God knows where. Fibber McGee and Molly... War of the Worlds... MY shows... makes you wonder who might be listening."

"Guess you've seen and heard it all in your day... OLDTIMER!"

Dan gave him a playful shove. "You may be a young punk, but your memory starts as far back as mine."

"You know more about this than me, man, but what I hear on the radio now... something's missing."

"THE HEART AND SOUL OF IT IS WHAT'S MISSING!" Dan said in a voice that boomed louder than what may have been prudent—one never knew who or what might be lurking in the desert.

"I remember staying up late to listen to Wolfman Jack."

"Broadcasting from XERF across the border—with no legal limits on the wattage those Mexican stations could crank out, they shot that program a good ways across the USA."

"He used to advertise all kinds of weird crap."

Dan got up to retrieve another brew from the cooler. He was animated now, an actor delivering his lines on an open-air stage. "Baby chicks by mail order—they were totally off the wall. Then, there was this guy in Chicago—Dick Biondi—craziest S.O.B. you ever heard. Those guys were PERSONALITIES. Now, you've got cookie cutter formats, and most of the voices you hear are just glorified card readers—except in the mornings where—even though they wouldn't consider themselves as such—formulaic bores trying to shock you with their tastelessness."

"So what happened?"

"Well, used to be that stations were owned by guys with a radio background."

"Makes sense to me."

"A lot of em came up through the ranks. A guy might have saved his money until he had the wherewithal to buy a small station somewhere. Maybe parlay that into another, and then another, until he was doing alright for himself. Point is, they KNEW the business. Somewhere along the line, big money investors took over. Most of them didn't know a damn thing about radio, except that they could turn a handsome profit by buying up stations, holding onto them for a while, then putting them back on the market to be gobbled up by some other fat cats. And that's pretty much where we stand today. A good-sized city will have thirty or more radio stations—but ever since deregulation, most all of them in any given market are controlled by a handful of conglomerates. The small independents—what's left of them—can't compete. They don't have the same dollars to spend on billboards, TV spots, or big prizes to lure listeners."

"So what you're saying is that greed won out, and maybe these fat cats don't really know what to put on the air..."

"They hire what are called 'consultants'—guys who DO have some radio background who go around touting themselves as experts. But as the number of individual companies owning radio stations declined, so did the number of consultants, until you had just a few of these high-profile guys calling the shots for the majority of the stations across the land. That's why you can go to Boston, Cleveland, or Denver and hear the same handful of formats with the same music, same sounding promos... same old same old."

Reno emitted an unladylike belch. "You know EVERYTHING, brother!"

"It only seems that way to you because there's so much you DON'T know," Dan said with a little needling laugh.

The two of them fell silent, gazing up at the stars. The wind blew cool upon their faces. In the dark beyond the campfire, nocturnal desert creatures approached, looked on with their ancient, instinctive dread of man, and melted back into the night.

Dan broke the spell by tossing his can in the direction of the burgeoning pile of empties beside the fire. "So now, I suppose, you want to know about political correctness and that whole can of worms."

"Sounds like the world's gone crazy."

Out of the corner of his eye, Dan saw the silver streak of a meteor, its brief shining moment played out against the black void of space. "On the surface of things, our peace and love movement won out—all men are brothers... we shall overcome... you're still so close to all of that in your mind. Now, we're sensitive to everyone's feelings, but it's insincere. It only applies to those segments of society that are large enough and organized enough to wield some power against you. We don't need to be politically correct toward the homeless because they have no power."

Immediately, as if to throw the statement back in his face, Dan flashed back to the outing with Gretchen on Fourth Avenue and the young panhandler he'd dismissed with a wave of his hand.

"My head is exploding, "Reno said.

"My head exploded back in '68."

"Congratulations, dude."

"Anyway, that brings us up to date... except for the computers. They run everything now, as I'm sure you've gathered, and they're all going to fail on the first of January."

"That's bad, huh."

"They're holding town hall meetings about it as we speak—all over the globe. I went to one. A self-proclaimed expert told us that martial law will be declared after the world erupts in chaos."

"You believe all that?"

"Nah... I don't think computers are going to do us in. We've survived until recently without the accursed things. Somehow, I think the best and brightest human brains will pull us through on that score. I'll tell you one thing, though, and I can't put my finger on it—but I feel a really weird vibe about this new millennium we're hurtling towards like a skydiver with a defective parachute..."

"Whoa... there's a wicked image."

"All the better that you'll be gittin' while the gittin's good."

Reno absentmindedly straightened his wig, a habit he'd fallen into back in what now passed for civilization. "Knowing how it's all going to turn out," he said, "how do I avoid a major bummer when I get back?"

"Uh, glad you brought that up. Gretchen (Dan winced at having to say her name) says you WON'T remember any of this. Once you return it'll be as if you never were here. Life will unfold for you the way it has for the rest of us—day by day—so nothing will come as such a shock, although the end result when you arrive again at this point in time may well be the same... a kind of vague disappointment."

The younger man considered this new wrinkle. "Yeah," he said finally." It'll be better that way—of course."

Dan stood suddenly and paced in front of the fire. He cleared his throat. "I-I want to go back with you, Reno. I NEED to go back. There's something I have to take care of."

Tranced out, Reno stared into the flames. He raised his head slowly, pursed his lips and said, "Awesome, dude... but I think it'll be up to that bunch of saucer jockeys."

And that's why I'll need you to help me convince them... deal?

"Okay old man, deal. If I make it that far."

Twenty-Six

Sid Kaplan called the meeting for 10 o'clock, immediately following the Dan Rivers show. The entire staff filed in, one by one—Stacy, Harry Dick, the sales crew, the young board operators who babysat the network shows that kicked in when Dan signed off.

Kaplan, looking old and tired, listed the reasons why he no longer had the energy to fight what had progressively become a losing battle. He introduced Mike Fallon as the new owner of the station.

Fallon said all the right things. There wouldn't be any mass firings. Everyone would be evaluated on his or her own merits. With all that corporate muscle in their corner, a new success story for KSUK radio was about to begin.

Dan, adept at interpreting upper management doublespeak, thought: That's great--he's going to pick us off one by one like a sniper holed up in a bell tower. He glanced over at Stacy and wondered how HER performance would be evaluated.

* * *

She sat at the edge of the pool, mesmerized by waves of sunlight zigzagging on the water.

Puerto Vallarta.

Stacy still couldn't believe that she was here. Mike Fallon was a mover, in more ways than one. Merely a week after his coup, he began the process of dazzling his new assistant. Since they'd be doing some travelling, he'd said he wanted her to get her feet wet. Get a feel for what business trips with her new boss would be like—though this diversion, it was emphasized, was purely for pleasure—a kind of celebratory sojourn.

During the morning, they'd taken in the sights--exploring the cobblestone streets of the "Old Town," then strolling along the breezy Malecon way beside Banderas Bay—inhaling the sea air and the vague piscatory smell that is characteristic of coastal villages.

Now, dangling her legs into the water, Stacy was indeed getting her feet wet in the pool adjoining the spacious villa—part of their upscale lodgings in the Marina Vallarta area, surrounded by luxury hotels, condominiums, and sailboats. Yes, Mike Fallon went first class. And if the idea was to sweep his young companion off her feet, it was certainly working.

She looked around and saw him enter the pool area. He was dark and toned in his pale blue swim trunks. He sat beside her and gazed into the water. "Ready to take the plunge?" he said.

Dinner that evening was in a fancy restaurant where someone—a maitre 'd or a waiter—is always hovering, catering to your every whim, as if waiting for you to drop your fork onto the floor so he can replace it forthwith. They would probably wipe your rear end for you, Stacy mused, if they figured you for a big tipper.

She recognized that it was the wine doing the thinking for her now. She felt like giggling. That might be inappropriate, but she'd been swept away by the glorious day and the attractive man gazing appreciatively upon her from across the table.

They were halfway through the meal when Fallon veered from the subject of tomorrow's activities (they were to rent a sailboat and cruise the bay—she'd heard that dolphins would swim right alongside the craft) to more personal matters. "You've never mentioned a boyfriend," he said. "I assume you have one."

Stacy looked down at her plate. "He's kind of an on-again-off-again boyfriend."

Fallon reached over and dribbled more wine into her half-empty glass. Shifting into "boss" mode, he said, "You know, the requirements of this job may place a strain on any such relationship." He paused for effect. "Just so you know what you're getting into."

She raised her head and met his gaze. The prudent and proper Stacy--sitting on one shoulder—whispered and told her not to say what she felt like saying. The brash party girl Stacy--swaying precariously atop the other shoulder with a drink in one hand and a joint in the other—told her to go ahead. "And what kind of a strain does it place on YOUR relationship?" she asked.

A momentary crack appeared in Fallon's veneer, and the look he shot her was a neon sign flashing the words NO TRESPASSING. Then he collected himself and said, "My wife and I have an understanding. Business is business... and business is requisite to a happy and prosperous home life—so we will put that to bed now... ummh?"

In the dream, she glided effortlessly underwater. She saw the hull of a craft overhead and instinctively knew that it was the boat she was riding on—or at least part of her was on—while the other part was content to shadow along like a mermaid. She had literally passed out upon hitting the sheets, and luxurious sheets they were in the queen-sized bed she had to herself—the boss ensconced in his connecting room—everything the way it should be in a working relationship.

The dream morphed into a nebulous romantic encounter. Someone was-melding into her like a spoon from behind. She turned to see who it was... and awoke from the dream.

"God... Mister Fallon... what's going on? What are you doing?"

Her head was still swimming—as it had been when she'd conked out.

Fallon draped his arm across her shoulder and his hand came to rest upon her breast. "I'm scared of the dark," he said in a mock child's voice. "Don't wanna sleep alone."

"Oh, Mister Fallon... you're crazy!" she said. Trying to be playful. Not wishing to offend him. The sudden sick feeling of that which had been repressed coming to the fore.

Through the fabric of the nightshirt, he gently massaged her nipple between his fingers. Stacy knew that there was a brief window of time that would provide the only opportunity to turn the situation in her favor and send him back to his room like the naughty little boy he was pretending to be. "You're a big boy now, Mister Fallon. Let's take you back to your bed and I'll tuck you in... okay?"

"Nooo... me hungry!" He lifted the edge of her shirt and took a peek at the black lace panties she wore. "Me wanna eat dat," he said.

"Mister Fallon, I can think of several reasons why this is not a good idea."

Yes, a number rational, logical reasons. And as she enumerated them one by one, Mike Fallon methodically slid the panties down her warm sun-baked thighs, down to her ankles, raising one dainty foot and then the other to slide them free.

This was the part where Xena Warrior Princess would have emitted that ungodly yipping noise—flip three times in the air—and upon landing, deliver a devastating blow to his nuts.

But Stacy liked men, basically. Liked them even though her sometimes boyfriend, Bruno, was a dork. Liked men even though she'd been used by them before—and she thought about that now—even as Fallon positioned his head between her legs, making retarded yum-yum sounds as he moved in for the kill.

She thought about the worst of them—the two drunken rednecks who'd picked her up while hitchhiking home from her high school graduation party. (Standing there by the side of the road, feeling like a woman ready to strike out into the world.) Climbing into the pickup with those guys. Sitting between them, knowing instinctively, but too late, that it was a bad move—the two of them with their high-pitched hysterical laughter saying, "WE GONNA POP YOUR PUSSY, SWEET THANG." And she, on the verge of panic, bargaining with them—in the end giving them blow jobs in exchange for her freedom.

Afterward, feeling too dirty, too cheap, and too guilty to tell anyone. She thought about this as Mike Fallon buried his face in her muff—knowing now that she was fucked—and still she liked men, basically, because she knew she didn't like women... and what else was there?

She thought about the time she'd tried out for the cheerleading squad but didn't make the final cut, as Fallon's tongue got busy activating her hot button... ooh... what mechanism was it in the brain that allowed the body to respond even when the mind was saying no? You can try to hold back but still, if the sonofabitch knows what he's doing... if he's an obvious EXPERT at it... if his tongue has trained with the masters as this tongue undoubtedly has... OOH... OOH!

All she'd ever wanted was to be accepted—and now this man, this powerful man wanted her to be his right hand, which was ironic, considering what he had just placed in her hand was growing and stiffening. He surfaced from his pearl diving expedition and hovered above her, waiting for her to put things in their proper place, which she did like the dutiful assistant—in fact, a full partner now in this endeavor. Rising to meet his first tentative thrusts, she thought of

Bruno and felt a stab of guilt—but only for a moment—as Fallon picked up the pace. She raised her knees to allow for maximum penetration, which really got him going.

UNHH... UNHH... UNHH... the slap-slap slapping sound as he slammed into her—and "Oh, Stacy—my sweet little Stacy... so tight."

And Stacy reaching behind to grab hold of the headboard to keep from being drilled right off the bed. "Oh... Mister Fallon... oh shit..."

"Call me... UNHH... UNHH... call me MIKE, Stacy."

"Are you... OOH... OOH... are you sure?"

"Yeah... UNHH... UNHH...what the hell... at least for tonight."

Twenty-Seven

Dan glared at her through the control room window. Even from a distance he could see that Stacy was glowing—and not solely due to the new tan she sported—as she manned her post, fielding phone calls with uncharacteristic cheer. Around the station the scuttlebutt was that she'd be getting her own office, soon as they could find a replacement at the reception desk.

But Stacy wasn't the only thing that was troubling Dan. Passing by the newsroom, he'd done a double take upon seeing a stranger sitting at Harry Dick's desk. On the way up front to query Stacy about it, he discovered the terse notice on the bulletin board: *Harold Dick has resigned his position with KSUK to pursue other endeavors. We wish him the best. Please welcome Joe Krueger from Louisiana to the news desk.*

Joe Krueger? From Louisiana?

"What happened with Dick?" he snapped. Dan was already mortified by Stacy's obvious capitulation to Fallon, and now this.

"Dick?" There was a dreamy look in her eye. "What dick?"

"Harry Dick! The guy who was our newsman the last time you and I showed up for work... remember?"

"Well, Dan... I guess he just decided to move on. Why don't you check with Mister Kirshbaum? Maybe he can tell you more."

"Kirshbaum? Who's Kirshbaum?"

"Our new General Manager. He's from Louisiana..."

"What the HELL is going on here—and why are we being invaded by people from Louisiana?"

He stormed off to his office and dialed Harry Dick's home number.

"Dick, here," said the voice at the other end of the line.

"Harry, it's Dan. Listen, this thing smells. I just want to know—"

"If I left of my own volition, that what you mean?"

"Yeah."

A loud protracted cough—legacy of the newsman's youthful nicotine addiction—caused Dan to drop the phone into his lap. When Harry was through hacking his guts up he said, "I was booted out on my BUTT! One of those unceremonious 'we're moving in a new direction' bits from this guy Kirshbloom—Christ, he just set foot in the place this morning. Guess Fallon needs a heavy to do his dirty work. Sure didn't waste any time."

"I'm sorry," Dan said. "What will you do now?"

"Well, I've still got my social security. I'll just have to cut down on a few things... like food."

"If there's anything I can do to help..."

"Aw, I'll be alright, Dan. Just watch your own ass now."

Dan's extension rang the moment he cradled the receiver. "Call for you from a Mister Jack Davis," Stacy said.

Puzzled, he scooped up the receiver again. The guy couldn't be calling just to talk about the weather.

"Remember that chickie?" Davis began. "That receptionist out here who was involved with Fallon way back when?" He gave Dan no opening to respond. "Well, I remembered something about her last night. First thing I remembered was her name. Doesn't matter of course. The point is, something she said to me one time popped into my head. We were making small talk and I started kidding her about Fallon—just to get a rise out of her... and she gave me this strange look. Then she says 'He's a FREAK, man.' Just like that."

Dan remained silent for a moment. Then he said, "Could have meant a number of things back then."

"Well, it was the WAY she said it. There was like... REVULSION in her voice. The next week she was outta there. Word was she'd quit, but—"

Dan cut the conversation short. "You're a good man, Charlie Brown," he said. Bolting from his chair, he headed up front. It was time for a serious word with Stacy.

But Stacy wasn't there.

He went into the control room where Hans, the board op, told him she'd gone to lunch, and that she was only working a half day and wouldn't be back. Hans began to bitch about her leaving him to answer the phones, but Dan was already halfway down the hall. Back in his office, he dialed Stacy's apartment. Please be there, he whispered. But after five rings, her recorded voice came on the line: *Wait for the beep... unless you're a creep.*

Exasperated, he left a message urging her to call him right away.

Stacy was aglow with the ambience of the casino. Like a solar cell, she was energized by the lights—and here in Sin City the neon glittered bright as the future she envisioned. It had been another of Mike Fallon's whirlwind, pick-up-and-go adventures, and she was learning to expect the unexpected.

A major broadcasting convention was taking place, and Stacy's presence was required for... well, she didn't know what for, but she wasn't asking questions.

They were staying at the Hilton due to its proximity to the Las Vegas Convention Center. "Next trip, we'll upgrade from this dump," he told her.

Imagine—calling the Hilton a dump... what an extraordinary man!

Fallon had peeled off a few crisp C-notes and slapped them into her palm—"pin money" for her amusement in the casino while he attended the evening seminars. He didn't give a damn about the latest trends in broadcasting, but it gave him a chance to schmooze with other bigwigs.

She fed coins into a number of one armed bandits as the electronic mayhem of row upon row of surrounding machines rendered a cacophony she found pleasing to the ear. She was enjoying herself, but couldn't help comparing this place to Tucson—or most of the casual, laid back west for that matter. And though it was now in the process of attempting to reinvent itself as some kind of Disneyesque theme park, there was a noticeably hard-edge to this town—as if the seed had been plucked from a gutter in the south Bronx by some giant hand and transplanted out here in the middle of nowhere-- nurtured and pissed on by Bacchus—golden showers turning to gold as it blossomed and grew into this glitzy island of light in the desert. She remembered that during her previous trip she'd seen a local story about a casino owner who had slapped a young TV news reporter across the face for asking a question the bigwig considered to be "uppity." That reporter left town a couple of weeks later.

She scoped out some of the other players. They weren't like the seedy looking slobs she'd rubbed elbows with—filling the room with cigarette smoke—at the low rent dive downtown where she and Bruno had bivouacked during her only previous visit to the city. This was an upscale crowd—most of them dressed to the nines—on their way to or returning from the big name headliner shows... and also satiating the place with smoke.

Earlier, Fallon had introduced her to a Mister Roy Lucas, who had joined them for dinner. Her boss had referred to him as a V.I.P. He was, in fact, one of Fallon's business partners from the midwest. She gauged Mister Lucas to be in his early sixties. He had a protruding belly that ran interference for him in a crowd. His sad eyes and sagging jowls reminded her of a Basset Hound.

He seemed like a kindly man.

It was nearly eleven o'clock when Fallon collected her from the casino. She could smell liquor on his breath. When they got to their room, he pulled her down onto the bed and smothered her with sloppy kisses.

"You're drunk, Mike," she said.

But not so drunk that he wasn't able to deftly remove her clothes. "I want you, Stacy," he mumbled, tugging at her black lace panties—the ones he liked and requested she wear when they were together. He slid one side and then the other free of her pretty feet. He entered her unceremoniously, a complete one-eighty from the patience he'd shown in Mexico, where he'd tuned her like a Formula One race car before sliding into the cockpit.

A sound came from inside the bathroom.

Stacy's head jerked in that direction. The door was closed. That didn't necessarily mean anything. But why would the water suddenly be running in the sink? Fear stabbed into her, as palpable as Fallon's knifing thrusts. "Mike," she said in an urgent whisper. "There's someone in... in THERE!'

Fallon was unfazed. He'd settled into a nice rhythm now, getting his groove on. "That's Roy... UNHH UNHH... he wanted to clean up a little before... OH—FUCKING GOOD GIRL... before returning to his hotel... so I gave him the extra key."

The door swung open and out stepped kindly old Mister Lucas. Frantic, Stacy groped for something she could use to cover herself, but the sheets were underneath her and the bedspread lay in a tangled heap down by her feet. And instead of the expected red-faced apology and hasty departure—Mister Lucas calmly pulled up a chair and sat down next to the bed. He watched them, nonchalantly, as though he'd just switched on the television.

Stacy hadn't felt this exposed since the age of twelve when her father walked in on her as she inspected her budding breasts in the bathroom mirror. Now, here was a much older man surveying her body, intruding on her most intimate moment. "Mike," she gasped. "We have to stop."

Fallon mumbled into her neck. "Baby... it's just you and me... you know I want you so much baby... nothing else matters."

He made his deposit, then opted for an early withdrawal, rolling off of her and onto his side—dead to the world. Stacy sat up and groped for the bedcovers. Mister Lucas rose from his chair and vaulted head-first onto the bed, effecting an awkward yet impressive somersault for a man of his years. He grabbed hold of her arms.

"Wake up, Mike... WAKE UP!" she cried.

Mike would put a stop to this. But he wasn't waking up. He wasn't even moving. Her instinct was to struggle, but Mister Lucas suddenly loosened his grip and said, "Stacy—don't be upset. It's only me... I'm not going to hurt you, I promise." He fumbled with his belt. "I'm Mike's partner. We share... everything."

She looked into his sad face as if trying to comprehend the incomprehensible—knowing that if she was going to muster up a fight, the moment was now. And in that naked moment, like other moments when something hangs in the balance—a moment stripped of all pretense—Stacy came to grips with why she was here, in this room, with these men, and she realized what she had become.

Mister Lucas fiddled with his fly.

Beside them, facing the opposite wall and feigning sleep, Mike Fallon listened, and felt a renewed stirring in his loins.

And as this decrepit and now disgusting creature mounted her, grateful as he was for sloppy seconds, Stacy—still sweet, and still a very young woman (at least temporally), softly... silently... began to cry.

Twenty-Eight

Agent Milburn stood before the white door with the big black knocker. He knew this was the residence of the woman who had driven Dan Rivers and his cohorts into the desert on the day of their suspicious meeting with the bib overalls guy, because he had tailed her—back to the mall, where she'd unloaded the others, and then to this ritzy pad.

He brought along a copy of The Watchtower, a booklet that nice Jehovah's Witness couple had left with him at home—before he'd dispatched them by stating he was a devotee of Madalyn Murray O'Hair. But that brief encounter had given him the inspiration for the role he would play today. Whatever it took, as long as he could pump this nubile female for information that might lead him to Reno Vegas.

A raven perched in a nearby tree seemed righteously pissed off by the intruder's presence, scolding him vociferously. Milburn looked up to see if the prudent thing to do would be to shield the top of his head and simultaneously took in an expanse of sky, a remarkably brilliant blue. Just another day in paradise.

While he vacillated between using the knocker or the bell, the door opened slowly, as if someone within had sensed his presence. And speaking of knockers. His eyes were immediately drawn to a perfectly matched set. Gretchen wore a pair of cutoff jeans and a T-shirt with nothing but her underneath. Her hair was damp and stringy, indicating she'd just emerged from the shower.

"May I help you sir7"

"Uh... yes, my child. Beautiful day, isn't it? God has blessed us indeed. I wonder if I might take a few minutes of your time..." He held the booklet up for her to see.

"Um... I guess so," she said. "But don't you usually travel in pairs? Husband and wife—that sort of thing?"

"Uh... my wife is dead. I mean she's sick. And near death. But I expect she'll be just fine."

She shrugged and ushered him inside like the caring and compassionate person she was becoming, day by day.

He sat on the overstuffed sofa and took a look around. Pretty impressive place. High ceilings. Casual yet elegant southwestern decor. He started thinking Mrs. Richbitch in the foothills, married to an attorney in all likelihood—past tense, no doubt, as there was no evidence of a male presence here—and evidence was Milburn's stock in trade.

"I can offer you water, juice, or tea," she said.

Or ME, he almost expected her to say—sitting there, looking at her perfectly rounded breasts, the nipples jutting like two hard pencil erasers. You'll go to hell for even POSSESSING a pair of tits like that, he thought.

He told her that water would be fine.

A conversation ensued, and Milburn tried to sound nonchalant as he made a tenuous segue from religion to the subject of UFOs. He tore his eyes away from her globes to study her face, but she gave nothing away.

"I think it must all be a big hoax, don't you?"

"Uh... yeah... mmmm... He was losing focus. Or more accurately, he had narrowed his focus and knew that he could be in trouble by becoming mesmerized by an object—in this case two objects—because it made him more susceptible to...

Gretchen watched as the nice man did a dead faint and toppled over onto his side. She knelt beside him and took his pulse. He seemed to be fine—just out cold. She'd taken note of the large bulge in his pants, which he'd tried to conceal by nervously crossing and uncrossing his legs. Her practical side took over, and that part of her was loathe to pass up a prime opportunity like this one.

Gingerly, she unzipped his fly, and wondered if it were possible to make an unconscious man come, but figured if anybody could do it, she'd be the one—knowing, with no sense of grandiosity, that she was the best that ever lived.

Slipping her hand inside his pants, she could feel that the man's shaft was still turgid. A very good sign. Time to get to work. Let's just see what we've got here. Gripping his erection in her accomplished fist, she maneuvered the head into daylight. A few rhythmic strokes and... OH MY GOODNESS! She dropped the pecker as if it had pricked her fingers, astonished by what she saw.

Twenty-Nine

Sondra worked, as certain people are prone to do. Reno had spent his days alone in the apartment--listening to the radio and watching music videos on TV—and getting depressed about the greed that seemed to permeate every facet of life. And the music... what happened to the thing that was closest to his heart?

BOY BANDS!

Those "manufactured" acts that all looked and sounded alike--doing the same dance steps—gyrating all over the stage like someone who desperately needs to find a restroom within the next fifteen seconds. There were no personalities any more—only "product." When did moves become more important than the integrity of the music?

Everybody wanted to be the Temptations. He could clue all of them in. You ain't the Temptations. You ain't never going to BE the Temptations. Don't even be tempted to THINK about the Temptations when you're out there, dude.

He could almost stomach the punk scene better than this. At least there was some honesty in getting up there and essentially giving the middle finger to the rest of the world.

Reno's pinky finger burrowed its way into his left nostril. Some people, when they needed to look within, contemplated their navels. When Reno was in a pensive mood, he'd go on a mining expedition.

Nose picking had become a lost art. That's because of all the gross-out things one could do, conducting a public excavation of your nasal passage was considered the most taboo. He couldn't understand why it was such a big hairy deal. People went out for pedicures, and that involved the jettisoning of some toe jam, did it not? Anyway, it was a matter of practicality. The "dry heat" Arizonans were always talking about meant the amount of boogerage one might encounter could be substantial.

He took a last glance around the apartment. Not so much to see if he'd forgotten anything—he didn't have much to keep track of—no, it was more of a silent goodbye. The time he'd spent here with Sondra welled up as a bittersweet memory. How could he say goodbye to... well... those JUGS? Those incredible, imposing, all engulfing hooters that shut out the light, the sound, and the danger of the outside world whenever his face was nestled between them. It wasn't just her body, though. Sondra was a cool chick on many levels, but it had become apparent—over the past couple of weeks—that bridging the gap between the space he lived in and the space where she resided was beyond his capabilities. That, and, as well as anything, he just got restless being holed up too long.

It was a short walk from her downtown apartment to the bus station. Better go before she gets home. He did some last minute primping in front of the bathroom mirror—straightening his wig and humming the tune to "Girls Just Want To Have Fun." A final salute to Jimi Hendrix on the wall, and once again he stepped out into a dangerous and unpredictable world.

To Reno's surprise, the annual Christmas parade was in full swing. Throngs of holiday fun seekers lined the streets. Little kids—some dressed as elves—sat astride the shoulders of dads and watched as the fire trucks, bedecked in white lights, trumpeted their way through the city streets, followed by antique cars filled with semi and barely famous politicians and local media personalities. Next in line, cadres of teenage girls decked out in red body suits, propelling their batons into the air—crouching here and there to retrieve the errant tosses that hit the ground. The world had changed, but Christmas was still Christmas, and Reno took some comfort in the thought.

Unfortunately, the bus station was still the bus station. A derelict was slumped against the wall next to the main entrance. He was engaged in an argument with an old hag (wife—mother—sister?) who tried to pull him upright by tugging on his arm, to no avail. Reno just hoped that the guy wasn't one of the drivers.

Till now, Derek and Sondra had seen to his needs, so he still had the same two hundred bucks that were in his wallet the night of the abduction. It wouldn't get him far, but it would get him away from here. He went inside and bought a ticket to Phoenix. On a bigger pizza, he could be a smaller anchovy--blending in with the mushrooms and the pepperoni.

He figured he'd better get something to eat before boarding the bus.

Awake. Disoriented. Sunrays slanting through a gap in the curtains that he now remembered wouldn't close completely. He got out of bed, took a piss, peeked out the window and realized it must be late afternoon, not morning light that greeted him.

Oh man—that bus. He summoned the memory of the young dickhead singing loudly—and off key—to the music on his CD player that only he could hear. An out of control toddler running up and down the aisle, plopping into the adjacent seat, then nodding off with his head in Reno's lap. A couple of ex-cons swapping prison stories. The rank odor of a fart from which there was no escape.

The romance of the road.

He dressed, donned his wig, and made his way down an outside corridor, searching for the ice machine. He looked up at the sign that read: Rock Glenn Motel. Below the name it advertised free cable and a heated pool. It wasn't the Ritz-Carlton, but the place was clean and off the beaten path, which was just where he wanted to be.

Turning a corner, he spotted the contraption he was looking for up ahead. A young, dark-haired woman stood in front of the machine. She didn't look much over five feet tall. The cubes made a clattering sound as they tumbled into her motel issue plastic tub. She turned and acknowledged him with a friendly hello. His eyes were drawn to her chest—though not for the usual reasons. Her baggy sweatshirt was emblazoned with the image of a clenched fist. Beneath it in bold lettering: YOU SUCK!

"Like your shirt, girl," Reno's cross-dressing alter ego exclaimed. He was getting his turn of the millennium vernacular down.

She thanked him/her with an impish grin. A real sloe-eyed cutie, this one.

"I'm Roberta," he said.

Her name was Alicia. She'd arrived earlier in the day. Traveling cross-country... in a roundabout way. No, she wasn't alone. Her "friend" was crashed out back in the room. They'd logged a lot of miles today. Sweet girl, though. And not too nosy about "Roberta's" story. Well, nice meeting you. Enjoy your stay. All that rot.

Reno returned to his room. For a long while, he sat on the bed and stared at the phone. He picked up the TV remote and flipped rapid-fire from one onscreen image to the next. Too bad that girl wasn't alone, Too bad that now we have all these channels and still not a damn thing on. With that, at least, he had grasped the common denominator of his era and the present day.

He woke with a start. These walls still so unfamiliar. He felt more like a fugitive than at any time since he'd bolted out the back door of that radio station and into Sondra's Camaro. He staggered into the bathroom to do his business. Too jittery to go back to bed, he donned his full distaff regalia. Even though his watch said it was nearly midnight, one couldn't be too cautious.

He undid the chain lock and cracked the door. The early December nighttime air was chilly—even if it was Phoenix. He stepped back and put on his heaviest flannel shirt—one of three stuffed inside his duffel bag. He circled the perimeter of the motel and arrived back at the office, which was darkened and locked down for the night. A walkway led to the center courtyard where the pool was located. Whoa—what was this? That churning sound meant someone was doing laps. He approached cautiously. A full moon provided the illumination he needed to recognize that shock of dark hair.

It was Alicia.

He stood at one end of the pool and kept silent. She back stroked fluidly toward him, and as she drew nearer a second, triangular shock of dark hair came into view. Oh my, the petite young thing was skinny dipping.

Thinking he'd better split before she saw him, Reno turned, then remembered that he too was a woman. He called out softly to her. She pulled up at the end of the pool and rested her elbows on the edge. "Hey... hi," she said. "I thought everyone in this place would be zonked by now."

"They are— but I couldn't sleep."

"Well, come on in. The water's really warm."

Sure thing, he thought. If only I could hide this noodle dangling between my legs. He uttered something about being too bashful, but pulled up a deck chair and the two of them, in low voices, jabbered away like old classmates. Alicia carried the conversation, her pert little titties submerging, then surfacing again in the water. Reno smiled as though he were hanging on every word, all the while thinking: I know a game... it's called "Bobbin' For Boobies!" Wanna play?

"You must think I'm a nut," she said. "That T-shirt... and now this."

"No—"

"I'm not belligerent—just the opposite. But there's a kind of purity in a statement like 'You suck!' Know what I mean?"

"Definitely," said Reno.

"There's no beating around the bush. It's like, okay asshole—you can read it, now prove me wrong... if you can."

Reno shifted nervously in his chair, watching her swim a few more laps and then pause for more girl talk.

"I was a computer programmer in Cleveland when I met Sergei. He asked me if I was happy. I had to think about it. He was into this whole Kerouac thing—the open road. He said you've got twenty four hours to make up your mind, if you want to choose freedom.., and that's how I learned it."

"Oh. Uh... what?"

"Non-attachment. It's like, a Buddhist thing. The root of all our pain is because we're attached to people and things. Ultimately, everyone and everything leaves us—one way or the other. We're here on this way station—planet Earth—in transit to somewhere else, so it only hurts to cling to things."

Suddenly, Reno's pining for his old life seemed trivial.

She clambered out of the pool and paraded past him, retrieving her towel from the back of a chair. There was nothing childlike about her rounded ass, pale and conspicuous in the moonlight. No, she was all woman. He wanted to reach for her, but she would surely think him to be a lesbian. She wrapped the towel around her body and Reno saw his chance slipping away like water cupped in your hands.

"I respected his honesty and straightforwardness," she added.

Sick with the anguish of his deception and what it was doing to him, Reno ripped the wig from his head and let it tumble to the concrete. "Fuck it!" he said.

Alicia glanced over her shoulder, then turned around and moved in closer to try to comprehend what she was seeing. "Wha—? You're... you're..."

"I'm a MAN, Alicia. I'm a man. Listening to you, I couldn't stand it any longer."

Her mouth hung open. "Okay... I get it. You're like... a drag queen. That's cool—my brother's gay too, man."

He heaved a sigh. He'd played the scene for maximum drama, but the audience had responded inappropriately. He looked down at his chest and the bra stuffed with cotton and shook his head. He could have left it there, but her words came back to haunt him. "I— I can't lie to you, Alicia. I'm not gay."

She placed her hands on her hips and stood there, as if needing time for this new reality to sink in. "You... you really got your jollies out here tonight then, didn't you?"

"Listen, I want to explain—"

But she was having none of it. She pivoted on her heel and stomped off, then wheeled around suddenly and gave him a clenched fist salute. "You SUCK, mister!"

Alone in the darkness of his room, Reno, finding it impossible to sleep, sadly stroked his weenie as he conjured up the haunting vision of Alicia's delectable derriere in the moonlight.

* * *

In the morning he peered from his window and saw them packing gear into their car. Sergei did exist—he was tall, and though he reminded Reno of a wire coat hanger stretched taught, the muscle shirt he wore displayed sinewy biceps. He possessed the smoldering countenance of the perennially pissed-off.

When they'd loaded up, Alicia's companion trekked toward the office while she rearranged some of their stuff in the rear of the hatchback. Reno saw his opening. He flung open his door and jogged over to her.

"What do YOU want?" she said wearily, continuing about her business.

Speaking at rap song pace, Reno explained that he had a lot of things to explain, and that he couldn't allow her to go off thinking him to be a butthole. He took a page from her own book and told her that she undoubtedly was getting attached to this guy and that she should dump him and the two of them could hit the road together.

Getting her first critical look at the male version of Roberta in daylight, Alicia pursed her lips and gave him the once over. "So what if I should get attached to you?"

He glanced nervously in the direction of the office. "Uh, we can deal with that later."

The impish grin she'd first shown him at the ice machine returned. "What the hell," she said. "You've already seen me naked."

"Get your stuff out of the car," he said.

"No need… it's my car."

Alicia's soon to be ex-companion, stuffing his pockets with English muffins from the free continental breakfast in the lobby, heard the banshee screech of tires as a vehicle spun out of the parking lot, prompting him to mutter something about people driving like assholes in this part of the country.

Thirty

And so, much like Sergei, a person she didn't know... yet, Sondra returned home to receive her rude awakening. She immediately phoned Gretchen to break the news that Reno was on the lam again. Her voice was measured, and, considering her fondness for the lad, remarkably composed. "He left a note," she said. "He doesn't seem to care about going back anymore. Said that living through the seventies, eighties, and nineties would be like sitting through a movie he's already seen—a lousy one at that. He's willing to take his chances."

Gretchen caught her breath audibly, and Sondra's voice went dead at the sound of it. "We HAVE to find him, Sondra. There's something important he doesn't know."

By the tone of Gretchen's voice, Sondra knew the news couldn't be good. Her reluctance to discuss the subject over the phone only added to the diminutive redhead's sense of foreboding as she down shifted her Camaro and turned into the driveway of Gretchen's on-loan estate. She still cared about the kid, even though he'd skipped out on her. Hell, he was like a son. A very naughty son who'd done naughty things to his "mom," but still...

Seated on the sofa where the slithery agent Milburn had effected his latest swoon, the two women sipped their tea. Gretchen eased into it. "I refrained from mentioning this to him so as not to add to his overall sense of anxiety—but now, circumstances have dictated that it be revealed."

Sondra sucked in a deep breath, held it, and squeezed her sphincter muscles tight, a technique she'd learned in a meditation class.

"Reno was transported into the future instantaneously, so time, in a sense, hasn't caught up with him yet. But there can be no denying that thirty years have passed between then and now. In a few weeks, I'd say, if he doesn't return to the year 1969, his body will begin to age at an abnormally rapid rate until he becomes what he rightfully should be at this stage—a middle-aged man in his fifties. It's just—"

"A matter of time?"

"So to speak, yes."

"The old story of the tortoise and the hare."

"With a different twist, yes."

Sondra had not considered such a scenario, and obviously, neither had Reno. An idea winged its way into her mind. If he stayed, she and Reno would be contemporaries. With the generation gap between them dissolved, there would be no barrier to a real and lasting relationship.

But that was a selfish thought. A horrible thought, really. One that she quickly brushed aside like a piece of dirt on her clothing. To lose all those years of his life—gone in a virtual instant—would be tragic. Not to mention that he'd still be little more than a teenager emotionally. "Whatever it takes—let's find him," she said.

Thirty-One

On their last night in Vegas, Mike Fallon informed Stacy that they were going to a party. She hadn't tattled on the old pervert Lucas, fearing that Fallon would misunderstand and blame her for the little "indiscretion." After all, had she actually fought the bastard it would have raised such a ruckus that anyone in the same room would have woken--even from a drunken stupor—and to try to explain to him what she still struggled to understand herself...

Anyway, the trip would end on a high note—literally. As their cab pulled up to the immaculately landscaped desert residence, far removed from the glitter of Las Vegas Boulevard, Stacy vowed to get her own glow on. She wanted to be nicely buzzed--though not to the point of where it would actually put her lights out.

Inside, a mixture of young to middle-aged sophisticates mulled around with drinks in their hands. Smooth jazz provided a silky undertone, the living room bathed in a low cast of purplish lighting that created a dream like effect. It felt like your typical cocktail party… until she spotted the guy with frizzy Richard Simmons hair sauntering around in his birthday suit.

He mingled with the other guests and they seemed to take no special notice of him. Stacy decided she would find something to drink sooner rather than later. Making quick work of the rum and Coke she'd mixed at the self-serve bar, she looked around for Fallon, but he was nowhere in sight.

DAMN HIM!

She didn't know a solitary soul here, and he was supposed to be her protector, though she was beginning to have her doubts about that. Well, if she had to track him down, she would.

The house was bigger than it had initially appeared. An indoor pool—WOW. A sliding glass door did what sliding glass doors do— it slid—and Stacy stepped through an open space, turning to thank the person who stood waiting for her to pass—a person who was also quite naked.

She gathered up a deck chair and fell into it. Bodies frolicked in the pool—some of them sans clothing—others more demurely attired in thong bikinis or speedos.

Stacy gulped her second drink.

Near one end of the pool, a tall cowboy type was holding forth with two young females. "I don't believe it," one of them cooed.

"I tell yuh, it's NINE inches... and change."

"Prove it," her companion teased.

Stacy couldn't discern what transpired then, as the women had closed in on him in a kind of mini football huddle. A moment later, their squeals of delight indicated that Tex had lived up to his billing.

Seeing no sign of the prodigal Fallon, she wandered back into the living quarters, past an open bedroom where a middle-aged woman with blonde streaks in her hair was doing an enthusiastic slurp slurp number on two younger men.

"Oh my!" Stacy exclaimed, at last grasping that this wasn't just a wild party—it was a bona fide SEX club. She wheeled around, careening into the Richard Simmons look-alike.

"COME here often?" he asked. "That's a joke. I can always spot the rookies... they tend to be a bit... overdressed."

Two women happened by and one of them said, "Is this guy bugging you?"

"Sexual harassment, BARRY," the other teased.

Barry's arms opened in a "Who, Me?" gesture, convincing no one of his innocence.

"I—I'm okay," Stacy said. "I'm just looking for—"

"Come with us, girl," the taller of the two women said as she locked arms with the new recruit. "We'll take care of you."

Stacy came to in a stupor. The last thing she remembered was downing several more drinks with the women, who didn't know Mike Fallon, they said—and even if they did, he wouldn't be using his real name HERE.

She looked down to find herself sprawled onto a bed with one of her new "friends" on either side, removing her clothes. "Whuz goin' on, you guys?"

"You passed out, kid. You don't want to barf all over your duds, do you?"

Then, before you could say "lickety-split," the taller blonde maneuvered into position and fastened her lips onto the yummy between Stacy's legs, while the shorter brunette caressed and fondled her breasts.

"Hey... you bitches are... GAY!"

"Not gay, baby," said the brunette. "Our husbands are around here somewhere. It's just that we swing both ways. Most of the gals here do. Hell, you get laid twice as much." Her lips settled onto the breast she cupped in her hand, gently biting and sucking the nipple.

Stacy felt butterflies in her stomach. "But I like MEN," she protested.

"So do WE!" the women chimed, quaking with the kind of contagious laughter that got Stacy caught up in it as well, though she wasn't sure whether to laugh or to cry.

"Hey," said the brunette, talking around the nipple still in her mouth, "if you want us to stop, just say the word. Rule number one of this club is that no means no."

But by this time, the blonde had zeroed in on the neophyte's nubbin, her tongue flicking up and down, from side to side, and in circular motions that sent waves of unexpected pleasure through Stacy's body. God, she thought, why were decisions becoming so difficult lately?

Two fire engine red-tipped fingers sank inside her. The bedroom door opened slowly, and a head poked its way inside.

It was Fallon.

He stood mute, hair mussed and a stupid-drunk grin on his face.

"You bastard," Stacy said weakly. She'd intended it to come out with more vehemence—after all, he was the one who'd led her into this life of depravity—but now, she was right on the verge.

Another head poked its way through the door. Ohmigod… it was Mister Lucas, grinning as stupidly as his partner in crime.

And then... and then the dam broke (and it was Hoover Dam no less), gushing unabated as the blonde brought her to the most intense, moaning, head thrashing from side to side orgasm of her life.

The audience broke into appreciative applause.

Thirty-Two

The morning man poked his head inside KSUK General Manager Kirshbaum's office. (There seemed to be a lot of poking going on everywhere these days.)

The GM wore a white shirt with a tie that looked like it was choking him. He could have been a used car salesman. "Sit down, Dan... I know we haven't had much chance to chat since I took over here, but I wanted to get you up to speed on a couple of things."

Dan looked around the room that Sid Kaplan had occupied for so many years. There was an austere feel to it, now that the old man's trophies and family photographs had been hauled away—like a museum with all the artifacts removed.

"We're making some on-air changes," Kirshbaum said, not one given to small talk. "We have a pet shop that wants to sponsor a lost parakeet report. They want to run it in your shift at 8:15—that's when the owner is usually listening. I guess he lost a bird at one time..."

Dan couldn't believe what he was hearing. He had his own opinion about pet shops and puppy mills, but knew that this was not the time to share it. "Uh... we ran missing pet reports before the changeover, but I can't remember anyone calling in a parakeet—not even once."

"That doesn't matter. You'll just read a live open to the effect of: 'And now the lost parakeet report—brought to you by Fuzzy Wuzzy—the home of all your fuzzy, furry, and feathered friends. We'll have the lost parakeet report in just a moment. Now, a word from our sponsor.' You read the live spot, then you come back and say: 'Well, folks—no lost parakeets today... isn't that great? Tune in again tomorrow at this time for the lost parakeet report, brought to you by Fuzzy Wuzzy, where you'll find Wagner's Bird Seed, the good stuff all the parakeets are talking about.' You get it?"

"What's to get?"

"Parakeets talk... get it?"

"Yes. Unfortunately."

Kirshbaum put on a false pouty face. "Hey, have fun with it, guy. The other thing is, we're dumping the network for the whole day following your morning show. We're going local."

"With what?"

"Bunch of preachers. Some guy peddling hearing aids. Multi-level marketing people making their pitches—that sort of thing. Hell, we'll put Ron Popeil on the air if he wants to buy the time."

Dan saw red. "Who's going to listen to that kind of crap?"

"Doesn't matter. They're buying the time—cash on the barrel. I'm not telling them that no one outside their immediate family will be listening.., and neither are you."

"Infomercials. Snake oil salesmen. So all you gotta do now is buy your way in, eh?"

"We already have people who've bought their way in, Dan. They're called thirty and sixty second commercial announcements. An infomercial is just an extended commercial."

"Yeah? Well what happened to the responsibility that broadcasters used to feel to put something entertaining on the air in between those spots? For the guy who's had a tough day at work and he's driving home in his car and he wants to turn on the radio and hear something he can relate to, or something that will make him laugh, or something poignant that will tug at his heartstrings... what about all that?"

Kirshbaum glared at him from across the expansive desk that all upper management types must have.

Dan glared back.

"You know who I work for, Dan. Case closed."

On the fifth day of saying, "Well, no lost parakeets today, folks," Dan lost it himself. "And you want to know why there are no lost parakeets?" he continued, diverting from the prepared script. "I'll tell you why... because you're holding them prisoner in little CAGES, that's why! Rare is the bird that is going to pull off a successful jailbreak—and if one ever does, you can forget about calling us because he ain't going to be hanging around your neighbor's birdbath... his little feathered ass is going to be halfway to Mexico before you can pick up the phone!"

The next morning, Dan played it straight again. He thought maybe he'd slid under the radar with his little outburst, since no one had mentioned it. Maybe the Fuzzy Wuzzy guy had been distracted—sitting on the can, or playing with his weasel—and missed the whole thing. But when he signed off at ten o'clock, word came down that Kirshbaum wanted to see him.

The GM was full of small talk this time. "How've you been feeling, Dan? Everything okay in your personal life?" He was acting too nice. Dan smelled a rat—that sinking feeling when you know something is coming, but all you can do is sit there with your thumb up your butt waiting for the bomb to drop.

Finally: "We're going to have to terminate you, Dan."

"It's about yesterday, isn't it?"

"Yes and no. The sponsor was *muy* pissed off, but your lapse in judgment only speeded up the wheels that were already turning. We've had someone with their eye on the morning slot for a while now. We just got them to sign the contract."

"Who is it?"

"Hey, I don't have to tell you, you know—you're already officially terminated—but I will... just to show you what a straight ahead guy I am. It's... a funeral parlor."

"A FUNERAL PARLOR? In morning drive... for FOUR hours?"

"They're going to pitch their caskets and burial plans, I guess. Take phone calls from the bereaved and show them what good deals they can get now that they're too distraught to think straight. Whatever the hell they want to do. We've grandfathered the parakeet thing in-- that's in the contract. People grieving for the dearly departed and their lost parakeets... Jesus, they go hand in hand. And frankly, this outfit is plunking down a pretty penny more than what your show was bringing in."

Dan got up and walked out because he knew that the other option— repositioning the guy's ass between his shoulder blades—wouldn't change anything."

Kirshbaum called after him. "You've got an hour to clean out your office!"

He went home. Tossed his briefcase onto the couch. Fuck it. There were plenty of other places to work. No, that wasn't quite true. After KSUK, there were basically four other companies that were calling the shots in the market. You no longer worked for a station. You worked for a multi-headed monster corporation.

He noticed the red light blinking on his answering machine. Thinking that Stacy must have gotten back to him at last, he pressed the play button and a voice from long ago, more frail sounding than he remembered, said, "Dan, this is Mary Muller in Iowa... give me a call when you can, please."

Mary Muller. Maya's mother.

He thought he'd make some dinner first. Or leaf through the TV Guide. Or maybe erase that message and pretend he'd never gotten it. Knowing that he wasn't going to do any of those things, he lifted the receiver and dialed the number that Maya's mother had given at the end of her message—area code plus the seven digits he still remembered after all this time.

There wasn't much for Mary Muller to say. Just that Maya had passed away the night before. Frozen to death in the middle of an Iowa cornfield. No, they had no clue as to why she would have ventured into the brutal winter night clad only in bedroom slippers and a nightgown.

"Maya had always been captivated by looking at the stars—you knew that, Dan—and maybe that's what she'd intended to do. She always loved you, Dan, in spite of everything. She never liked to talk about those days, but a mother knows. A mother always knows."

South Tucson. Textbook example of urban decay, where the billboards are in Spanish and likely as not the retort of gunfire can be heard in the distance—or close by, for that matter--on any given night. But on this occasion, as Dan wheeled into the parking lot of the Hell Hole Bar, it seemed as though the shooters were taking a holiday--it being so close to Christmas and all—as televisions glowed eerily--like spaceships—in darkened rooms, and cartoon characters waxed poetically about peace on Earth.

He had a drink. Hard liquor wasn't his thing, but he wasn't going for style points. He had another. And another.

A young woman sat in repose down at the end of the bar. She smiled when he glanced in her direction. She was pretty in a used up sort of way. The second time he caught her eye, she got up and planted herself onto the stool beside him.

"Looking for a date, *mi amor?*"

"Don't tell me... you're just an old fashioned girl who's feeling a little lonely tonight."

She laughed agreeably, revealing a missing front tooth. She wasn't pretending to be anything but what she was. "What you want, my love?"

"I wanna 'nother drink.'

"Buy me one too... then we go fuckie."

Sitting in his car in the darkened lot behind the bar, the young lady demonstrated her expertise in the art of localized massage. "Whassa matter, baby? She asked.

"Dunno."

"I know how to wake you up." She laid her head in his lap and went to work. After a few minutes of what must have been one of her more heroic efforts, she surfaced for air and said, "Your noodle is dead, man."

"Forget about it then," he said. "I'll give you an extra ten bucks for your trouble."

She went into a pout, turning away from him. "You shame me and you shame my heritage."

"What... hell you mean?"

"You don't like *latinas*."

"You're fulla shit—I like all kindsa women."

"You know what I do to guys who don't like Mexican girls? I sock 'em in da balls!" And with that she turned and WHUMP—delivered a solid hammer strike between his legs.

"FUCKING BITCH!" he roared, doubling up with the pain. "Get the fuck outta my car!"

He reached across and yanked open the passenger door, placed both feet against her ribcage and gave a mighty shove that sent her sprawling into the dirt.

She came back like a wildcat, jamming her middle finger in his face. "Fuck YOU, man! You're OLD, and you need Viagra." She was shouting now. "Hey everybody—this white piece of shit can't get it up!"

"Cool it," he said, or I'll tell your mother you nibble on men's pee-pees in the back of cheesy bars."

"My MUDDER? Ha! She's the one got me into dis bizness."

"Yeah, well... I fucked her and there's something you didn't know."
He forced his voice into its deepest Darth Vader register. "I AM
YOUR FATHER!"

"You're crazy, man." She kicked the car door—once for spite and
once for good measure. Gathering a loogie from deep in her throat,
she let it fly.

Dan had reached over to grasp the door handle when the chippie
scorned had started in with her Rockette impersonation and managed
to pull it shut just as the mega-glob splattered the window and
dribbled down in delicate stalactite fingers of spit. She stomped off
toward Sixth Avenue, leaving him to curse and collect himself.

"Don't expect a Christmas card from me, sweetheart," he muttered to
no one.

Knowing that he was too whacked to drive, Dan poured himself from
the vehicle. He considered returning to the bar when a figure emerged
from the darkness, accompanied by a familiar clackety sound. Some
derelict, wheeling a black dog in the basket of a hijacked supermarket
shopping cart. The man, wearing a railroad engineer's cap, veered to
avoid the unexpected obstacle in his path, which displayed the
wobbly gait of an obvious drunk. "What the crap you doin' out here,
mister?"

"Same as you, Dan said. "Taking the wife out for a stroll."

The man looked down at his dog. "No... but she does bear a striking
resemblance to my FIRST wife."

Dan guffawed. He tendered the sawbuck he'd fished out of his wallet
earlier to placate the hooker. "Here then. Buy your gal some food."

The dog's ears pricked up.

The man waved it off. "She's got plenty to eat. We're just makin' a cigarette run."

He tried to stuff the bill into the fellow's overalls pocket. "Ya gotta promise me you won't blow it on booze."

The man stepped back. "Excuse ME—but only ONE of us is shit-faced here, and it ain't yours truly. By the way, I'd zip my fly if I was you, 'less you want to freeze the best part of you."

Dan's chin dropped as he inspected himself. "Fuck it," he said, waving his arm in dismissal. He tottered off toward The Hell Hole.

"Hey mister," the man called. "You're under ARREST!"

Dan looked around at where Rusty—the homeless guy who had just placed him under citizen's arrest—hung his hat. It was a pup tent set up in a wash running through an area that was the city—but not of the city—untouched as yet by the rapacious hand of development.

Dan had never been arrested by a homeless person before (how many could make that claim?), but this night would be one for the books either way.

Rusty and his "old lady" had a small cooking fire going. The coffee was hot and black—and like a harsh dose of reality, it tasted bitter. As some of the cognitive functions of his brain returned, Dan recognized that the man had steered him clear of the streets for his own good. But as the effects of the booze wore off, the pain ebbed back in. Dan buried his face in his hands and sobbed.

Rusty's dog licked his ear.

The woman, gaunt and hard looking beyond her years, cradled him in her arms.

"Let it out, hon," she said. "Whatever it is, get it off your chest so it can't hurt you no more."

"I feel like a fool," he spluttered. "You guys are homeless and I'm losing it over MY problems."

Rusty motioned toward some nearby trees. "Are the birds homeless?" he said. "All a matter of perspective."

"I... I caused the death of someone I loved."

The woman glanced at her man, then back down at the troubled stranger and said, "Whatever you've done, God will forgive you."

"Maybe God's more forgiving than I am... I'll NEVER get rid of this... never!"

Rusty touched his arm. "Look at me, man," he said. "All you can see is a street person, but that's 'cause you're lookin' with your eyes. You can't see everything that way. You gotta look with your heart to see that when a man's with the ones he loves, he's home. You gotta figure out who it is that's in your heart *now*—then go and be with that person, 'cause it's the only thing that matters. The past is dead and gone. Seems to me the only real sin is not bein' able to learn from our mistakes."

The woman spoke again. "Is there someone like that, hon... someone you want to be with?"

Dan felt something that had been wound tight begin to unravel inside him. He nodded slowly.

"Then looks to me," Rusty said, "like you gotta choose between a live person and a dead one."

Thirty-Three

Stacy, at her desk, was in the middle of a daydream when the phone rang. She was thinking about the roomy new office being prepared for her—and the title she would carry—"Executive Assistant to Mr. Fallon."

Movin' on up. Well, by God, she'd earned it.

The voice on the phone sounded vaguely familiar--asking for Dan Rivers. She gave the caller the carefully worded company spiel: "Mister Rivers is no longer with KSUK. He has opted to pursue other endeavors. Beyond that, all employee information is confidential."

When the caller hung up, Stacy slipped back into her reverie. Yeah, I made it the old fashioned way, she thought with a twinge of bitterness... the OLDEST way.

Arriving home from her meeting, Sondra checked the phone messages—and there it was—pay dirt! Reno's voice, sounding like an apologetic but obstinate little boy who'd run away from home. No, he didn't intend to come back, but he wanted her to know that she'd done nothing wrong. His words melted into the background as she busied herself writing down the phone number from her Caller ID display. Yes, she had mentioned it once to him in passing, briefly explaining how the device worked, but he obviously hadn't taken it into account, and why would he? There likely was some perv out there right now, someone who HADN'T been catapulted thirty years into the future, making an obscene phone call from his home phone—oblivious to the likelihood of Caller ID because a stroke (or rather, a number of them) had turned his brain to mush.

Sondra wasted no time in dialing the number. Thanks, kid," she said. "We may be able to save you yet.'

❋ ❋ ❋

Dan pressed each number in sequence again. It was his second try. He'd panicked in the middle of the first attempt. This time he steeled himself and allowed the call to go through. A voice he didn't immediately recognize said hello. What if she had moved out— moved on to a new location? "Hi, er… maybe I have the wrong number. I'm trying to reach… Gretchen?"

"She's not in. This is Brigitta—may I help you?"

He nearly dropped the phone as the memory of that embarrassing night returned. He sat for a moment in stunned silence.

"Who's calling please?"

He thought he'd make up a name. Pretend to be one of Gretchen's clients eager to get his rocks off. Then he sighed and said, "It's me… Dan."

"HI DAYAAAN," Brigitta cooed. She's away for a few days. I'm taking care of the place."

Smacking noises resonated in his ear. Good God, she was eating. "Where'd she go?" he asked.

"Not supposed to (smack, slurp) tell."

"Great."

"Dan?"

"Yes."

It sure would be nice to see you ag—"

Click.

* * *

Stacy had her new office. She had her more than generous salary hike. But being "kicked upstairs" had made her feel isolated. She was used to being the first thing they laid eyes on upon entering the building. And it was precisely because she was no longer the centerpiece of the KSUK studios that she stood peering down the hail, eyes narrowed to slits and murder in her heart.

Mike Fallon was immersed in a cozy chat with Candice, the new receptionist.

Stacy's replacement.

Moments later she watched from her window as the two of them got into his car and drove off. She knew what he would say later on--that he had taken the new girl to lunch just to make her feel welcome. That's how it starts, she told herself.

That's how it all begins.

Thirty-Four

Agent Milburn phoned detective Almorzado and told him the Reno Vegas flap was an obvious hoax, and that the Bureau was dropping its investigation. Almorzado, who'd given Reno up for dead years ago, was happy to concur, and to put the matter to rest again in his own mind. Milburn hadn't lied about the Bureau—he just left out the part about his own unofficial "inquiry."

Now, he stood back and admired his handiwork. The aging panel truck, which he'd recently considered getting rid of, had, via his artistic skills, been transformed into the flagship of ELMER'S EXTERMINATING—emblazoned prominently in black on either side. Below, in smaller lettering, it read: *The best in the west at eliminating desert pests.*

Hell, it ran well--there was nothing wrong with the motor--and now with a fresh coat of paint you couldn't tell it from any other commercial vehicle on the road. All that was left to do now was to load up the essentials—hunting rifle, handcuffs, etc.—and he'd be ready to roll, blending in with the scenery like all those air conditioner repairmen and commercial carpet cleaners.

Fuck the termites. He was after bigger game, and those two prick teasers were going to lead him to it. Pity they knew too much, because now "Elmer" would have to eliminate them too.

Alicia drove while Reno spilled the whole fantastic, spaced-out story of aliens, time travel, and the whacked out FBI agent that was hot on his tail, but had most likely lost the scent by now. He didn't know what she'd make of it so he fell silent to give her a chance to weigh in.

"Jesus," she said after a moment. "I've taken up with a time-displaced transvestite who's run afoul of the law. Get out of my car right now."

Reno took this to be a rhetorical statement, since she was doing 75 and wasn't slowing down.

Later she said, "I see danger ahead for you, bub. But you can hang with me until the end of the line."

"Where's that?"

"Sedona. I feel that I'm being led—by who or what I don't know. Maybe just psychic intuition. I'm looking for a sign. When I find it, I'll know what's next."

"I didn't think a gal like you would be totally without direction."

"You've told me you don't care, but still I feel the direction YOU'RE heading in is back—back to where you came from. You're journey is a metaphor."

"Don't go too profound on me, dude."

"You know, it's the same road we're all on—trying to get back to The Source. The well from which we sprang. Some of us know that's where we're headed. Most don't. They're caught up in the seemingly endless cycle of birth and death. Wheel turning round and round..."

"Umm... I think I've heard that song since I've been in this decade."

"Steely Dan. And there's a Beatles tune, 'The Long and Winding Road.' I wasn't around when that came out, but some songs are timeless. Anyway, it's all just a dream the Supreme Being is having.

Nothing really dies because we're not real—we only exist in his imagination."

"Nothing dies?"

"Nothing dies but the dream."

"Yeah, but... what if it's a really BEAUTIFUL dream?"

She reached over and swatted him on the back of the head. "That's for calling me DUDE!" She grinned, then positioned her elbow on the headrest and slowly stroked his wig. "I'm not letting you in my pants," she said. "Getting attached to someone whose future is so... up in the air, shall we say, would be a bonehead move for me."

Reno didn't know how to counter this, so he went silent.

"Maybe you're thinking you could hit it once, twice and be done," she continued, "but that's not how it would be. You'd like it too much. All the guys like it too much."

"ALL the guys?"

"Not as many as you're thinking, bub. It's just that I've been told I'm hot stuff. You'd burn your fingers, little boy."

"Oh, man."

"You know me enough to know how I talk."

"Yeah, but why get me stirred up? It's been bad enough thinkin' about you back in the pool."

"This sex thing keeps rearing its little purple head."

"Not too ladylike of me, I know."

"Hey, I know you're horny. You're a guy. A YOUNG guy. That's why I give you permission to take care of yourself. Just don't splatter the windshield so's I can't see where I'm going."

Thirty-Five

Gretchen guided the Jetta into a parking spot in front of the café. The sign above the door read: *HOG HEAVEN--come on in make a pig of yourself.* They were somewhere between Phoenix and Flagstaff; and they'd decided to stop because neither of them had eaten before setting out.

Sondra said, "This is it, huh?"

Her companion, who didn't get out of Tucson much (except for an occasional interplanetary business trip), tended to regard one establishment as pretty much like another. But Sondra understood that once you ventured outside the state's metropolitan areas, it was a whole different ball game.

As the women emerged from their vehicle, a pickup truck came barreling into the dirt and gravel parking area, kicking up a ton of dust. The truck jerked to a halt and the driver, wearing a white cowboy hat, said to his passenger, "Lookit the udders on thet one, Jimmy—we oughta take her out to the barn an' hook her up to the milkin' machine!"

His companion, sporting a black cowboy hat, gave his crotch a tug and said, "Jay-ZUSS! Lookit the face on thet chinky-lookin' one—I'd rather hook her up to THIS, Darrel."

The driver gave his own jewels a squeeze in solidarity.

Inside, Sondra and Gretchen inspected the menu. There were numerous entrees befitting the place's name. Pork chops. Pork tenderloin. Ham and eggs. Ham and cheese sandwich. Ham salad.

Each similar entry was denoted by a smiling cartoon pig caricature to the left of the name. The scent of roasting meat filled the air.

A gum-chewing waitress came to take their orders before they'd had any reasonable time to decide. She told them she'd be right back. Then, in classic waitress fashion, she disappeared—never to be seen again.

The cowboys ambled in. Neither of them looked older than twenty-five. They slid into the adjacent booth. The one facing the women caught Gretchen's eye and tipped his hat. The other dusty range rider fiddled idly with packets of sugar and sugar substitutes, poking holes in some of them with a dirty fingernail.

"Don't fergit, we gotta castrate thet bull tomorrow," said Mister White Hat in a voice that carried throughout the corridors of Hog Heaven,

Gretchen decided she was no longer hungry.

Out of the blue, a different waitress appeared and ministered to the cowboys. After a minute she returned with two icy cold beers and plopped them down on the women's table. Before they could protest, the waitress gestured toward the adjacent booth and said, "Your friends sent these over."

"Let's go," said Gretchen, "I don't want to eat any pigs and I don't want to deal with any-"

Too late. The men were standing beside them. Gretchen found herself eyeball to belt buckle—a big silver one—with Mister Black Hat. But she wasn't interested in any cowboy crotch—except in a purely clinical way—and this was neither the time nor the place.

"Beg pardon, ladies," said Mister White Hat. "We thought you might like to join us..."

Sondra, older and more worldly (as opposed to otherworldly), took control. "We don't drink and drive," she said, as politely as she could muster.

"Uh... sure, that makes sense," said Mister Black Hat. "Where you ladies headed, anyway?"

"West," Sondra lied.

Black Hat looked at White Hat and grinned. "Thet sure narrows it down—don't it, Darrel?"

"Look," said Sondra. "We've had a death in the family and we're going to a funeral. Otherwise we'd be a lot more hospitable, know what I mean?"

The men tipped their hats. "We're sorry for your loss," they said in unison. (They both watched police dramas on TV and that's what the cops automatically said to any and all grieving individuals.)

Then Black Hat said, "Guess you won't mind if we take these brewskis back."

On their way out the door, Gretchen congratulated Sondra on her quick thinking. Emerging into the bright sunlight, each of them scanned the parking lot, casually, before piling into the car. Neither took any special notice of the panel truck with Elmer's Exterminating emblazoned on the side, sitting there amongst the other vehicles as innocuously as bird droppings on a post.

They pulled into a rest stop off I-17. Many are called, but the call of nature is the most insistent of all. Not wishing to lose valuable time, they thought they'd do their business, stretch a little, and hit the road again.

Sondra dropped some coins into a vending machine and bought two cans of soda and a couple of candy bars. They would need at least some token nourishment for the remainder of the trip. The women strolled to a grassy area and sat at one of the accommodating picnic tables. A sign read: *Poisonous Snakes and Insects Inhabit the Area.*

Gretchen ruminated on how many in-transit butts from all over the world (indeed the galaxy—now that SHE was here) had occupied this same spot. It's a humbling kind of feeling to realize that in the end, what links us together is not our minds, but that part of the anatomy that makes contact with the park bench, the bar stool, the public toilet seat. And, at the very moment when she was reflecting on the subject of asses, Mister Black Hat and Mister White Hat arrived in their pickup.

"There they are!" said Mister Black.

"Geez, you think we shoulda followed 'em all this way?" asked Mister White. "What makes ya think they'll be nicer to us now?"

"Tell you one thing—there ain't no funeral out here in the middle of nowhere. Why, they was puttin' us on." Mister Black spat in the dirt. "You cain't always break a filly on the first try, but with a little sweet talkin' I'll bet we can coax 'em into that gully over there—then it's RODEO time, boy!"

"YAHOO! Let's git after 'em."

They started across the grassy expanse that lay between the parking and the picnic area. Then a voice, which sounded to them ol' boys like it came right out of the sky, boomed: "THIS IS THE VOICE OF GOD. LEAVE THOSE BITCHES ALONE OR I'LL MAKE YOUR PECKERS FALL OFF!"

The cowboys froze in place, as if they had suddenly pulled up lame, and looked around warily. They saw no one. Nothing but the two accounted for vehicles in the lot.

The voice thundered again: "I SAID THIS IS GOD, GODDAMNIT... YOU COWPOKES DEAF OR SOMETHING?"

"Jesus, Darryl," said Mister Black. "He means us."

"GET BACK IN YOUR TRUCK AND LAY RUBBER... THIS IS YOUR FINAL WARNING."

"Holy shit, Darryl—he's gonna punish us for thinkin' impure thoughts of them that's in their hour of need. Dunno about you, but I like my tallywhacker just the way it is!"

Clutching their hats with one hand and their crotches with the other, Mister White and Mister Black made a mad Le Mans scramble for their truck. (Years down the road, they would point to this day as the catalyst of their religious conversion—their wives and nappy headed children being spared some of the details, of course.)

Across the way, Sondra turned to Gretchen and said, "Did you hear someone shouting? Sounded like a loudspeaker but I couldn't make out the words."

In his panel truck, hidden from view behind the rest area's expansive and well-appointed brick shithouse, agent Milburn clicked off his microphone and grinned sardonically. Back at Hog Heaven, he'd watched the cowboys take out after the women, so he tailed along in tandem. Noticing a sign for the rest stop six miles ahead, he gambled that the babes would be exiting there. Gunning it, he passed both vehicles, giving himself the lead time he needed to set up. Years ago he'd outfitted his truck with the mic and loudspeaker, thinking he might someday need to use it in the line of duty. *Get out of the car with your hands up*—that sort of thing.

Had it been necessary, he would have confronted those boys at gunpoint—but luckily "God" was on his side. Nobody was getting to those two prick teasers before he did—at the appropriate time, of course—though he knew in his gut that the rest of the game wouldn't be nearly such a slam-dunk.

* * *

The desk clerk at the Rock Glenn Motel—a kid barely out of high school—tucked away the porn mag he was perusing when the two women came through the door. Yes, he told them, a shorthaired blonde—a real looker—had checked in, stayed overnight, and checked out. No, she'd given no indication of her ultimate destination.

Dead end.

Outside, they took stock of the situation. Dejected, Sondra offered that Reno could be anywhere by now.

A man came around the corner of the building—a high-rise kind of man in a single story world. He walked in a hunched up manner, as if he were leaning into a cold wind, but the breeze was calm. He passed the women... stopped... then turned around and went back to talk to them, "You look lost," he said. "Or maybe YOU lose something?"

"No, we're fine," Sondra said, taking Gretchen by the arm and urging her toward the car. Neither of them cared for a repeat of Hog Heaven.

"I lose somebody," the man said.

"We're sorry for your loss," Sondra responded over her shoulder. "We have to go now."

"I lose my girl. Throws my bag into parking lot and takes off. Leaves me flat and I don't know why. Only thing—met some girly boy the night before—you know, man looking like woman. I make joke about it in the morning after she tells me..."

Gretchen and Sondra had reached their car, ready to slam the doors on one more annoying pussy hound. Suddenly, the scene looked like a video being run in fast motion reverse as they scrambled out of their seats and charged the man like a couple of shameless groupies—as if they feared he might duck into a waiting limousine.

As if he had someplace else to go.

"Reno!" she cried, as the splendor of Sedona unfolded before them. "LOOK!"

"Yeah, they call this Red Rock country. I was here a couple of times... back when. Better than the Grand Canyon to me. I mean, that's big and all—but this place kinda casts a spell on you."

As they drove, Alicia craned to take in the eerily shaped buttes, mesas, and spires—dotted with juniper and pinon near the base--morphing into shades of vermilion and beige as they rose to meet the imposing blue sky. Inevitably, they caught up to a tour bus spewing black smoke out its blowhole. "Shit, roll up the windows," she said.

"That's the trouble with a place like this, dude. Everybody wants a piece of it."

"Everybody wants a piece, period."

They followed route 179 to uptown Sedona, passing trendy hillside galleries, boutiques, and assorted small shops along the way. They stopped to poke around in some of the shops, which were glitzy and overpriced. Reno held a small glass figurine of a bear in his hand. He turned it upside down to look at the price tag. Seventy-five dollars.

Alicia remarked that that was excessive even by turn of the millennium standards. "I wonder where all the hippies are," she said. "You know—the *beautiful people*."

He gave her a wry look. "Probably somewhere hiding out from the tourists."

Rolling again, Alicia looked to her left and spotted the Red Planet Diner. Intrigued, she wheeled into the parking lot and pulled up next to the flying saucer fountain in front of the place. Water cascaded from a hole in the middle of the "craft."

Reno gazed at the novelty and was transfixed.

Alicia got out of the car and peered inside the place, which was not yet open for business. A sign inside read: *Earthlings—Please Wait to be Seated.*

When she came back, Reno was still staring at the saucer.

He tried to distract himself by flipping through the TV channels while Alicia took her shower. Earlier, he'd gazed into the bathroom mirror, and it seemed that he was looking older, somehow--or a little worn down at least. Maybe the stress and anxiety of the mess he was in was taking its toll. Yeah, that had to be it. Well, there were advantages to being a woman—just apply a little make up and he'd be good as new.

Propped up in the motel bed the two of them would share—for the sake of economy only—he considered the irony of the situation. He'd never shared a bed with a woman he hadn't put it to (mom excepted, of course), but the chances of connubial bliss with Alicia were about as slim as gnat's pecker.

Don't think he hadn't considered opening that door and stepping under the warm shower stream with her, the steam rising around them as they soaped each other down. But that would be forcing the issue—something he didn't want to do—and with that tack came the likely possibility of outright rejection and an unpleasant scene.

Like it or not, he needed her. A stranger, seemingly chosen at random, with no logical way for anyone who might be looking for him to link the two of them together.

He thumbed through the Tucson newspaper they'd picked up from a stand that had today's editions from both metropolitan areas, wondering if there might still be something in there about him. An item about a coyote—or illegal alien smuggler—being apprehended by the Border Patrol caught his eye. His mouth fell open when he read the name: Derek Johansen.

Jesus—old Derek! He'd thought of his former mentor as being wise in certain ways—when it came to assessing other people's situations— he just wasn't shrewd enough to keep his own ass out of a sling.

Too bad, man. He shuddered to think that there could have been an "accomplice" named Reno caught in that snare as well.

He pushed his pinky finger up inside his left nostril. Some people liked to contemplate their navels, but Reno knew that with the "dry heat" Arizonans were always talking about, the amount of boogerage one had to contend with could be substantial.

Alicia emerged clad in a one-piece thermal underwear type getup with a trap door in the rear that conveniently unbuttoned when you had to take care of business. The kind of thing some crusty old farmer—not an enchanting young woman—might wear. The outfit was bright orange--totally chic, he thought sarcastically—better suited to go traipsing around in the woods with the hunters.

She was sending him a message, and he read it loud and clear. "Nice pajamas," he said.

"Like them? They're the latest thing from Paris." She settled in beside him and burrowed beneath the covers, leaving only her pretty head exposed. Turning on her side to face him she said, "Tomorrow's a big day. We're going to hit the vortexes, and I'm expecting nothing less than a mystical experience."

"The guidebook says they're energy centers—but what's supposed to happen?"

"Uh, you know… psychic stuff. The paranormal." She was getting sleepy now. "We'll… just have to see… what happens."

Sergei jerked out of his road-induced stupor. "That's her car!" he ejaculated.

It was just after 10 p.m. and the three of them had cruised virtually every street in Sedona—pulling discreetly in and out of motel parking lots, as the Russian scanned the vehicles waiting like patient steeds for their owners to return and guide them a little further down the trail.

Having zeroed in on the place where Reno and his new companion were holed up—doing God knows what--Gretchen and Sondra agreed that now was not the time for hasty moves. The stray cat may be cornered, but coaxing him into your cage could still be a formidable task.

A stakeout would be best. They would hunker down in the car, sleeping in shifts, with someone keeping an eye on Alicia's vehicle at all times—though they understood that all was likely to be quiet on the western front until morning.

Gretchen, drawing first watch, gazed up at the full moon. Nearby, agent Milburn, conducting his stakeout of the stakeout, was also drawn to the glowing orb—thinking his own thoughts, which, one might assume, would be vastly different from those of Gretchen.

But in fact, they were remarkably similar.

Thirty-Six

The sun rose over the world. Sondra had zonked out in the back, but with dawn's early light she righted herself, rubbed the back of her stiff neck, and squinted into the front seats. Gretchen was still out of it on the driver's side, and Sergei, In the passenger seat was... SHIT! The Russian, who was supposed to have manned the third shift, should have been awake and at least semi-alert—but he was a long snoring log of dead weight.

Sondra glanced at her watch. It was already 7:30. She looked for Alicia's car and saw an empty parking space. "Son of a bitch," she murmured.

Gretchen woke and looked at the useless heap beside her with its eyes closed, head tilted back, mouth agape. She turned to her comrade in the back seat.

"They're gone," Sondra said.

Gretchen looked at Sergei, then back to Sondra. They both looked at Sergei again and read each other's minds.

"Do it," Sondra implored.

Gretchen reached over and poured the contents of her water bottle into his gaping pie hole. He woke, coughing and spluttering.

Sondra shook her head. "That's what happens when you trust somebody," she said, feeling let down by yet another man.

"Sergei," Gretchen said, "you told us your friend wanted to visit a vortex site."

"Yuh... vortex."

"Which one?"

"Dunno. She not decide, last I see her."

"There must be some tourist info on these locations in the motel lobby," Sondra said. She scrambled out of the car. "Be right back."

Sergei, still in his sleep-induced fog, fell against the door and managed to haul himself up into the crisp morning air. "Gotta pee," he said, and tottered off toward a hedgerow beside the motel.

A minute later, Sondra returned with a fistful of pamphlets and said, "I've got maps."

"How many spots?" Gretchen asked.

"Four. We need to pick one and go."

Gretchen nodded toward the building. "He's still over there somewhere."

"We know what the woman's car looks like and we've got the plate number. I don't mean to sound callous, but time is of the essence... fuck him."

Sergei tucked himself back inside his zipper and was making his way back when he heard the now too familiar sound of screeching tires. "Oh shit," he said. Not again!"

Agent Milburn had discreetly tailed the young couple to Cathedral Rock trail, but his ascent was marred by a group of neo-hippies making the trek back down. Their high-pitched giggling was a dead giveaway—the bastards were stoned out of their gourds. Subversive scum! Not worth the powder to blow 'em to hell—that's what he'd said as a young man during the anti-war turmoil, and that's what he still said today. And even though it was a new generation, bloodlines were bloodlines. Scum was scum.

A dude with dreadlocks lost his footing for a moment and bumped into the agent as they squeezed past each other on the footpath. Just a graze, really, and the kid mumbled "sorry." But that wasn't going to be good enough. Not by a long shot. Milburn toted his rifle in its case, but he also had a loaded 357 Magnum tucked inside his waistband.

It happened so quickly that everyone gasped. Grabbing the perceived offender by the arm, he pressed the gun barrel flush against the youth's head. "You want to fuck with me, boy?" he said, his voice skewing into a maniacal register.

The kid's disbelieving companions piped up with a chorus of "Hey, c'mon man," and "Whoa, chill out, dude!"

Then, as quickly as he had lost it, the fuming fed regained control and stepped back. He lowered the weapon and fished his badge out of his shirt pocket, holding it at arm's length for each of them to see. "Federal agent," he said, in his best Joe Friday monotone. "Official business. We have a report of some criminal activity in this area. You kids take off. Beat it."

The idea of plugging one of them in the butt as they as they high-tailed it out of there—just for laughs—was tempting. But it was time to take care of business. He gazed up at the imposing rock formation and smiled.

With nothing logical to go on, Sondra decided they would take the vortex areas in alphabetical order—hoping that Reno and his new companion would do the same. That meant the Airport Mesa location first. Then Bell Rock, Boynton Canyon, and Cathedral Rock. They gunned it down 89A to Airport Road.

Headed tragically in the wrong direction.

Sergei attempted to thumb a ride, but the early morning motorists regarded him as a piece of trash beside the road. Perhaps it was fitting, then, that he eventually managed to flag down a garbage truck.

The driver, who had finished his morning rounds and was now off duty, listened to the Russian's description of his two former traveling companions. If they could catch up to those hotties. Sergei insinuated, there'd be one for each of them.

"Climb aboard," said the captain of the slop ship.

"Stinks in here," said Sergei.

"Ha—try riding in back."

***

The trail fanned out into a rocky plateau. Reno breathed in the winter morning air and gazed up at the edifice towering a thousand feet into the air. Cathedral Rock. Before his eyes, it turned into a rocket berthed at its launch pad, ready to blast off into space.

Alicia took in same sight and, to her dismay, could not shake the image of an erect penis.

Agent Lawrence Milburn, now halfway up the trail, looked up and saw the shape of his own face, ala Mount Rushmore.

Reno and Alicia selected a large flat-topped boulder and sat on it to meditate—oblivious to their fate.

Milburn continued his plodding journey, slouching toward Bethlehem.

On their way to the Airport Vortex, Gretchen slammed on the brakes. "What are you doing?" Sondra asked.

"I'm turning around. Call it a hunch, but Sergei mentioned that the girl was spiritually oriented—we're heading for Cathedral Rock."

Meanwhile, back at the ranch, Sergei and the salivating sanitation guy (already with visions of nooky dancing in his head) spotted the two women heading in the opposite direction.

"It's them!" Sergei shouted.

The hulking mass of steel made a sharp U-turn, nearly toppling over in the process—spilling excess coffee grounds and cat shit out its rear end.

"Follow those BEETCHES!" the jilted emigre exhorted.

Thirty-Seven

Agent Milburn tottered up the last few feet of the trail. He spotted his quarry immediately upon entering the clearing. Side by side they sat, roughly a hundred yards away. No one else around, and that meant no witnesses. He crept behind a large boulder and steadied his binoculars. Ha! The unsuspecting fools had their eyes closed. Reno would never know what hit him.

Silently, he removed his rifle from its case.

Gretchen and Sondra clambered up the trail.

Sergei and the garbage truck driver were not far behind. Hurling the occasional epithet in their direction, Sergei wanted the women to know he wasn't pleased with them.

The garbage guy, with a size fifteen spare tire around his middle, fell gradually behind the others until he eventually lost sight of them. He said fuck it and collapsed in a heap in the middle of the trail.

Milburn took aim, getting a bead on Reno. He was enough of a "sportsman," or at least considered himself as such (as well as possessing an egotistical confidence in his abilities), to eschew the use of a telescopic sight. But he had a stationary target—how could he miss? "Adios, time-travel man," he whispered.

Reno felt something zing past his ear, and a split-second later he and Alicia heard the report of the rifle. Their eyes met in astonishment, but only for a moment, as instinct took over and they scrambled down from their perch, taking refuge behind the mass of rock.

"Shit!" said Milburn, acknowledging the near miss.

"Shit!" said Reno and Alicia in unison.

"Shit!" said the garbage guy, who possessed a truer kinship with the word than any of the others, as he tried to right himself from his prone position halfway down the trail.

Milburn stood to survey the situation, and in doing so revealed himself to the trio of Sergei, Sondra, and Gretchen, who'd heard the shot moments before entering the clearing.

Sondra sensed immediately what was going down. "RENO," she called. "Wherever you are, stay put!"

Milburn whirled and trained his weapon on the intruders. "Get over here," he ordered, "and keep your hands where I can see 'em." He kept the rifle aimed in their direction and forced them to sit with their hands behind their heads. He flashed his badge at arm's length, as he had done with the hippies.

They were close enough now for Gretchen to recognize the man she had taken for a missionary that day in her living room. "Holy moly," she said under her breath, remembering the secret she'd discovered inside his shorts.

"You cannot hold us like this," Sergei said indignantly. "I am American citizen now… I know my rights."

The former muscovite's accent was all too obvious. "What have we here?" Milburn said. "A genuine RUSSKY?" He spat into the dirt. "Commie bastard."

"Commie bastard?" Sergei whined. Have you not heard of glasnost my friend?"

`EVIL EMPIRE!" the government agent bellowed like a country preacher. EVIL EMPIRE!"

Sergei leaned into Sondra and said, "This man is crazy."

Meanwhile, Reno and Alicia—having picked up on Sondra's warning--watched the scene that was unfolding and sensed that their stalker might now be distracted. They decided to make a break for it and put more distance between themselves and the shooter.

"You cannot cover all five of us," Sergei piped up again. "Some will get away and alert police."

Milburn, realizing he'd lost sight of his original objective, whirled again and spotted two figures in motion. He took quick aim and squeezed off a shot.

One of the figures dropped like a marionette gone limp.

Thirty-Eight

Alicia had been running slightly ahead and to the left of Reno, and he saw her fall. He crouched over her body and looked into her lifeless eyes. 'NO!" he sobbed. NO!"

The others ran toward them as if in a dream—Milbun casting his rifle aside to join in. They crouched around the body—each horrified, including the perpetrator himself, at least for the moment.

Heads turned in succession-- eyes focused upon the killer. They moved on him as one. Backtracking, the agent drew the weapon tucked inside his waistband. "You assholes are forgetting who holds the cards here," he said. He knew he could hold off the three of them. Wait… three? Someone was missing.

The redhead.

He took a quick glance over his shoulder. She was gone all right— sprinting down that trail, no doubt, to seek out the local authorities. The situation demanded a quick assessment. A man in his position could talk his way out of one dead body, but FOUR—that would bring on some major heat-- and would any of it be worth the scrutiny he'd be placed under?

The answer, he decided, was no. That meant taking prisoners. He'd march the three of them back down that trail—double time—and beat it out of there before the carrot-top (she couldn't have that big of a lead at this point) could return with the gumshoes. Anyway, he had Reno—that was the main thing.

He had Reno.

Sondra literally ran into the garbage guy (or Sanitation Engineer as he preferred to be called) as she careened down Cathedral Rock trail—slipping and skidding and almost taking a tumble a few times along the way.

He was poking along, heading back to level terrain after deep-sixing the idea of ever completing the semi-vertical journey. He thought he'd met up with an escapee from the looney bin when she grabbed hold of him and shouted, MURDER! MURDER! She shoved him in the back and, like a high school cheerleader, exhorted him to GO! GO! GO!

The garbage dude (whose name, it should be mentioned here, was Billy—because nobody likes to be recognized only in relation to refuse) kicked it into a gear he never knew he had and rumbled down the footpath like a blocking fullback ready to knock someone on his ass.

Upon reaching the trailhead, Sondra remembered that Gretchen still possessed the car keys, and that the cell phone was locked inside the Jetta. "Your wheels!" she said to Billy, who stood hands on hips, gulping air. They boarded the hulking crap wagon, which was, by the way, now overdue at the terminal. Billy turned the key to start her up.

"Damn!"

What a time to get temperamental. She'd given him no trouble early this morning. He tried it a few more times.

"What do we do now?" Sondra asked.

"Let 'er sit a minute."

"We may not have a minute to sit."

But that's what they did. They sat. More like a Nogales than a New York minute. Billy tried the ignition again and this time the engine awoke. He was about to shift her into gear when something moved into the field of his peripheral vision. He turned and looked straight down the barrel of agent Milburn's gun.

Thirty-Nine

Reno took a look around. It was dark inside this place, whatever and wherever it was. A bare concrete floor was not the most comfortable resting spot, but it beat riding prone and tied up in the back of Milburn's panel truck, the five of them packed in like so much cordwood.

His eyes began to focus and he recognized it as a garage, maybe—no, it was bigger than that—a warehouse of some kind, or what used to serve as one, with the look and smell of a structure long abandoned. Add to that the pungent aroma wafting from the rear of the garbage truck, which was being detained along with the others inside the walls of this spooky place, and it became abundantly clear that they weren't being lodged at the Hilton.

Milburn was nowhere to be seen.

Sunlight slanted dimly through a small louvered opening directly above the structure's massive wooden doors. The Russian was up and had already cased the joint. He stood in one corner, appraising a couple of rusted oil drums anchored in cobweb. Hearing Reno stir, he turned and said, "I already push hard against doors. Must be bolted from outside. Help me move one of these things and I stand on top to get a look outside."

"There's a road," he said, balanced precariously on the drum. "It's dirt. I see what's left of another building... just a couple of walls... and a big, what you call tumble wheel, I think."

"Tumbleweed," Reno corrected. He looked at Gretchen, who had gotten to her feet and was listening to Sergei's eyewitness report.

It's a ghost town," she said. "It won't do us any good to yell."

Billy stood in silence, vowing never in his life to pick up another hitchhiker. He couldn't believe the chain of events that had culminated in some crazed fanatic ordering him to follow along behind, under threat that he would first blow the brains out of his hostages, then track the fat boy down and make it a clean sweep. Under those circumstances, he could think of nothing to do but comply.

Yes, he knew they were in the middle of nowhere, or at best, the edge of somewhere—even though he was from the area and felt a certain twinge of guilt in not being able to give the others a clue as to their whereabouts. Milburn had purposely led him on a wild goose chase, twisting and turning and doubling back to create a maze of confusion before leading him down the nondescript dirt road to the location he must have (and indeed had, quite by chance during an earlier unrelated trip to the area) discovered in advance--a place where people who had gotten in the way and knew too much for their own good could easily disappear off the face of the earth.

Sondra came over and put her arm around her friend. They both knew that they must soon follow through with the unpleasant task of informing Reno of his impending date with middle age. Considering their predicament, it couldn't come at a worse time.

But they would hold off on that little duty for a while, as over the next several days, Reno would descend into a funk of despondency —saying little or nothing at all to the others, staring at the walls and thinking of Alicia—blaming himself for her terrible and untimely demise.

The body of the woman that had been discovered near Cathedral Rock was the lead news story on the local Sedona, Cottonwood, and Prescott radio stations. Near the end of the newscasts there was also the curious item about the overdue and presumed missing in action garbage truck and its driver. People get knocked off all the time, but a big shit wagon disappearing into thin air--that's a story.

In the days to come—as no trace of the vehicle or its attendant were found—the story overshadowed that of the young murder victim and spread throughout the state. Then, it got picked up by the national media—one of those quirky items they like to seize upon from time to time. Peter Jennings, Dan Rather, and the rest of the talking heads prompted nationwide speculation as to whether the driver might have been leading a double life and was faking his own death. Or—and this was the more fascinating idea—that the truck had been beamed aboard a UFO, ostensibly because the aliens wanted to study our methods of trash collection.

Forty

Agent Milburn was at an impasse. Damned if he did and screwed if he didn't. Let the detainees go and they would surely implicate him in the death of that girl. Make them disappear permanently and the temperature would be turned way up, especially since that radio guy—the wild card in all of this—was aware of his overriding interest in Reno Vegas.

Ah, Reno. It could have been so easy too, had he only managed to isolate the pot smoking, acid dropping, peace loving, guitar playing, hippie chick balling jerk—a person who technically did not exist to begin with.

Milburn didn't think of himself as an evil person, just a man with a job to do—so in the meantime he brought the prisoners food from the burger joints and provided them with coffee cans to do their business in. But as the days passed, the malodorous task of emptying and replacing those receptacles demanded that a decision be made posthaste.

Drive a couple hundred miles north of Tucson and you're still in Arizona, but for all practical purposes it's another world. The higher elevations bring snow in the wintertime, and the shut-ins were feeling the chill of a proverbial long winter's night. They'd been supplied with some army blankets—another of Milburn's "humanitarian" gestures, which provided some buffer against the cold and a thin layer of padding between flesh and concrete slab. (The dilemma was to determine whether to use it as a mattress or a blanket, and some tried to do both, encased like mummies from the neck down.) Most slept fitfully, arranging and rearranging their carcasses in futile attempts to find that comfort zone.

Gretchen slept hardly at all. Awake one early morning, she sat propped against the wall, trying to remember if it was Friday or Saturday, when a rat squeezed underneath the doors and crept around inside the building, curiously inspecting its human inhabitants. The hulking silhouette of the garbage truck was like an elephant standing sentinel in the darkness. Had it been a real pachyderm, it surely would have reacted to the rodent's desultory inspection.

Accustomed as she was to wiggling and squirming things, Gretchen harbored no fear or loathing for the creature. She had half a hamburger stowed away. Breaking off a piece, she tossed it toward the rat, which made quick work of the offering. The rodent stood on its hind legs, and though it didn't come any closer, it peered expectantly in her direction. She tossed another piece.

There was something in the urgency with which the varmint ate that was reminiscent of her estranged lover's dog, Harvey. She thought of the affection she'd felt for the pooch--which was regarded as a "pet." Then she looked at the rat and the first word that came to mind was "vermin." Something to be avoided, or exterminated when necessary. She pictured Harv in her mind, then looked again at the rat—and it dawned on her.

They were both God's creatures.

Gretchen remembered the revulsion she'd felt back at Hog Heaven, and in a sudden flash of illumination, understood that Harvey, the rat, the pig, the cow, the songbird... they were ALL God's creatures—and they were fundamentally the same.

Forty-One

"Alright, pay attention," he demanded. Milburn leaned against the big truck's hood—his weapon trained on the prisoners. They sat elbow to elbow like obedient school children on the floor below him. "I'm opening this up for discussion. The question is... what should I do with you assholes?"

They looked at each other with raised eyebrows. Billy, who had piloted the great behemoth of *basura*, which stood useless and dejected like a decommissioned battleship, was now considered "missing in action." Patrons along his route in the Sedona area had begun tying yellow ribbons around their curbside trash receptacles in hopes that one of their own, a noble warrior who had fought the good fight for freedom from olfactory offense, would return home safely. Who can say, but it was likely that now he felt the vibration of that outpouring of love, and so became the first to respond by saying, "Uh... why doncha let us go?"

"Yeah, let us go!" the others chimed in, as if that were the obvious solution.

Milburn smiled. "Just like that, eh?"

"Yeah, and uh... we'll all sign a statement saying we never saw the guy who did the shooting," said Billy. "Fact is, I never did. And... my wife's a NOTARY."

Sondra couldn't hold it in. Half delirious with apprehension and anxiety, she burst out laughing. And despite their predicament, the others, including their captor, joined in—momentarily dispelling the tension.

The moment passed.

"So… I'll just get a pen and paper and we'll draw something up, and then Fat Boy here can drive us to his place and have the little lady affix her stamp to the document, and you all can have your lives back."

"Heh heh… uh… YEAH!" said Billy.

"NOT!" said Milburn.

It was around noon, as Dan was driving home from a dog food run to the market, that he felt a chill inching up the back of his neck. It made him shudder. He had experienced such moments before throughout his lifetime, and they usually didn't amount to anything— no premonition of doom or disaster.

This time was different.

A picture was taking shape in his mind. A blurry picture, but he could make out one form, and it was that of Gretchen. He could see that she was in distress. Indeed, he could FEEL that something was wrong. Dreadfully wrong. It was the feeling of cold, clammy fear.

Then he remembered what she had told him—eons ago, or so it seemed—about her telepathic abilities. Her extraterrestrial ancestors had the real power, but owing to the fact she was a hybrid, her gift was diminished. Spotty at best, and not to be relied on. But it was there, and she had said that if ever she really needed him, she'd concentrate real hard and send a message.

The shudder coursed through his body again and he saw her face, enveloped in a fog. She seemed to be speaking to him. Not words, exactly... more like one particular word being spelled out.

He tried to read her lips.

* * *

Gretchen had sensed that things were about to take a turn for the worse. She saw it in the religious fanatic turned bizarro government agent's eye—that deranged look she'd observed back at Cathedral Rock. She conjured up a mental picture of Dan and projected a thought stream out into the universe. Slowly and silently she repeated the letters: S-E-D-O-N-A. It was all she could do—not knowing exactly where they were, but she had estimated the time they'd been riding in Milburn' s vehicle to be about half an hour, which meant they couldn't be terribly far from the new age Mecca.

Milburn sighed. He waved his gun in the air to get their attention. "In for a penny, in for a pound," he said." Five assholes and six bullets... that leaves one to spare. How nice."

"I am not an asshole, sir," came the lone dissenting voice. It was the Russian popping off again. "I am American citizen, and you are agent of the United States government. I know because the others tell me this. You are disgrace to this country, sir."

A collective catching of breath came from the silent majority, and someone muttered, "Oh, my God."

Milburn smiled. He pointed his weapon directly at Sergei's head. "Well, my fine foreign devil," he said. "Here's what I'm going to do for you. I'm bestowing upon you the privilege of being first to die. And while two of these assholes over here are spreading your butt cheeks, I'll be inserting the barrel of this gun into YOUR poop chute and pulling the trigger. We'll SEE who's the asshole then."

He scanned each face before him, looking for their reactions. When his eyes fell upon Gretchen, she appeared to be in a trance, though her lips were moving.

"What are you doing, sister?" he said mockingly. "Praying?"

Gretchen jerked out of her trance. Their eyes locked, and once engaged, it was impossible for any man to tear away from her gaze, which was a mistake for Milburn. He felt an immediate stirring in his loins. "Get over here," he said, motioning with his weapon.

She came to him. "Lift your shirt," he demanded.

"Leave her alone, goddamnit!" This time it was Reno who had mustered his bravado.

"Shut up!" snapped the man who held all the cards. "Unless you'd like to trade places with the Red Menace over here."

He turned back to Gretchen. "Lift it, I said."

She did as she was told, and, sans bra as usual, her exquisite breasts popped into view, the nipples at full attention like the guards at Buckingham Palace. This was an embarrassment for her—they always seemed to be hard, regardless of any sexual excitation, especially when exposed to the elements.

Out of respect, Reno and the Russian averted their gazes.

Billy, however, had never drawn to a pair like this in his life, and he was awe struck. A fly flew in and out of his gaping pie hole. He didn't notice.

Milburn felt the crotch of his pants tighten—the breathing room that normally was there had been sucked out. He lined up the gun barrel with her left breast and slid the bore down over her erect nipple until it disappeared into that black hole of annihilation.

Fascinated by his own ingenuity, he moved on to the other glorious globe and repeated the procedure.

The feel of cold steel made her nipples harden all the more.

But while he was playing this little game with his symbolic phallus, the agent's God given member had swollen to mythic proportions—a transformation that was not lost on Sondra, gazing up at the spectacular erection about to burst through the fabric of his pants.

Unfortunately for Milburn, it felt like all the blood was rushing to his penis, leaving too little for his brain, and he felt a blackout coming on—just as it had during his initial encounter with the exotic beauty. He felt himself slipping into another narcoleptic nap, and there was nothing he could do about it.

He collapsed in a heap on the floor.

Gretchen's image began to fade like a TV picture deteriorating into "snow." Dan looked at the letters he'd written down—the ones he thought her lips had been forming. F-E-D-O-R-A.

Fedora?

Who in the hell had a fedora, and what significance would it have for him to begin with? His mind became a motor that would turn for a moment but wouldn't start, as he reached for possible meanings.

There were none, but he couldn't shake the notion that Gretchen was in some kind of trouble.

Big trouble.

He knew what he would have to do, distasteful as it might be. He would call Brigitta again and demand that she inform him of her friend's whereabouts.

Half an hour later, he found himself staring at the big black knocker on the mammoth white door of the rambling stucco house. And despite the knowledge of what was behind that door, he would stay the course, for Gretchen's sake. For the sake of a memory, if nothing else.

Brigitta had gotten the upper hand again, insisting that the phone wasn't safe and that he would need to come over to get the information he wanted. Seeing her again was like scratching your ass and discovering that painful boil you thought you'd gotten rid of has reappeared.

He took a deep breath and rapped on the door.

She wore a loose fitting kimono. It was black—the color that's supposed to de-emphasize one's girth—but it wasn't fooling him. It anything, she looked like she'd gained more weight—at least twenty-five pounds since the horrible and embarrassing night Gretchen had "introduced" him to her.

They sat on opposite sides of the coffee table. Brigitta crossed her immense thighs of cellulite. "Had lunch yet, Dan?" she purred.

"Yes... yes, I'm fine," he said. "Couldn't eat another bite."

"Well... you wouldn't want to leave without DESSERT, now would you?" She lifted the kimono, uncrossed her legs, and there it was in all of its bewhiskered glory—the RANKEST RIP this side of the Rio

Grande. There was no avoiding it. Like a gaping gorge one must bound to get to the other side of the river, this would be the price he would have to pay. He supposed he could whomp on her ass to get what he needed, but she was Gretchen's friend—and he was not a man prone to violence.

"I'll only need you for a few minutes," she giggled. "You're that good, Dan."

Oh, God... who had he screwed over in another lifetime to deserve this? Once, he was a child. A fair-haired lad racing gleefully through open meadows rife with the scent of yellow and purple flowers— believing with every fiber of his being that life was good, and that he would grow up and find that special girl—who'd be nothing less than an angel, and... fuck all that. A man's gotta do what a man's gotta do.

Grimacing as he regarded the fathomless fur pie, Dan held his nose and dived in.

* * *

Nobody moved. Shocked by this sudden turn of events, they stared at the man lying in a lump on the floor--still clutching the gun in one hand, but otherwise dead to the world. Then, as if a starter's pistol had gone off, they were on him. Check his pockets, someone said. Look for keys. Yes, here they are—two of them on a ring. Try them in the padlock that secures the doors. Shit! None of them fit.

"Wait a minute," said Billy. "Those are the ignition keys to my truck!"

"And that's all he's got on him," Sondra said. "Which means he locked himself in here with us. He must've removed whatever normally bolts the doors from the outside, and engaged that padlock to secure them from the inside right after he entered. Either he planned to kill us and save the last bullet for himself, or he's just a bumbling sonofabitch."

"Don't matter," said the redcap of rubbish, "we're bustin' out of here!"

The truck's innards were slow to crank, as it had been sitting idle for several days. "Come on baby," Billy coaxed. "COME ON!"

The big engine roared, finally, like the MGM lion in a cranky mood. At the helm once again, Captain Billy—who didn't know he was Catholic—crossed himself and floored it. The gigantic stench transport smashed through the big warehouse doors and sent them flying like they were toothpicks.

* * *

At home, Dan tried to remove a certain nasty aftertaste with repeated brushings and half a bottle of mouthwash. At least his latest "performance" with Brigitta had netted him all the information she was privy to—that Gretchen and Sondra had set off for Sedona in search of Reno (he could be forgiven for misreading lips— FEDORA... duh...), which was something, if not a lot, to go on.

As he saw it now, there was only one option left. He loaded Harvey into the car and the two of them headed out into the desert. The nice neighbor lady who normally looked in on his furry bedmate (the only one he had of late) if Dan was going to be absent for a day or two was out of town, and there was no time to make other arrangements. They were going to be partners in this adventure—that's just the way it had to be.

Forty-Two

When they arrived at Cletus's place, a locked gate prevented them from entering the driveway. A hand-lettered no trespassing sign with the third "s" missing warned of the recluse's mistrust of strangers. Dan beeped the horn a few times and eventually the big guy, clad in his trademark bib overalls, ambled down the driveway—shotgun in hand. The big man squinted and frowned until he got close enough to recognize the face in the car. One of them anyway. He unlocked the gate and motioned for the visitors to pull through.

Dan noticed right off the bat that a new garage had been erected next to the cabin. The doors were closed so he couldn't see what was housed inside, but the building appeared more than adequate for Cletus's pickup truck and any tools he might be storing. Overly adequate and then some. Once inside the cabin, Dan understood why.

The Greys had arrived—which, in fact, was what he was hoping for.

Willie and a few of the "boys" were seated around the kitchen table. They were finishing up one bottle of wine and starting on another. Dan was introduced. Harvey took one look at the aliens and barked his head off.

"Bad manners, Harv," Dan chided, though he was just as incredulous at the sight of them. Knowing that extraterrestrials exist is one thing, but meeting up with them is quite another.

Willie stood. He appeared to be as in awe of this exotic species as the dog was of him. He'd seen the coyotes that skulked around Cletus's property at a distance and knew what they were, but this was his first "close encounter." Motioning with one spindly finger, he said, "Bring the canine companion forward."

Cletus assented with a nod and Dan cradled his squirming, fussing buddy in his arms. Harv looked up into Willie's enormous black eyes. Willie stared back and seemed to be communicating—telepathically, no doubt—with the animal. After a long moment, Harv strained forward and licked the alien's face. Willie giggled like any Earth kid when a slobbery tongue slavers his nose (except that Willie didn't have what we would think of as a nose). His laugh sounded like the trill of a warbler strained through a fifties Japanese transistor radio speaker.

Dan spilled his story. Willie's face showed a look of consternation when he learned that the earthling they had earlier agreed to transport back through the time warp had disappeared, and that the lovely Gretchen, (of whom the Greys were most fond) was also missing—and possibly in trouble. He pledged his assistance in the effort to locate the pair.

Willie said he knew the "gang" that had originally abducted Reno, and that they were a rogue bunch, highly prone to screwing things up. They had pulled this kind of trick before—snatching a prim and proper woman from nineteenth century England and dumping her off in a Hell's Angels compound in California. She was lucky to survive the debauchery.

There was a pause in the conversation. Willie looked at Dan expectantly.

Something else was on the earthling's mind. It was easy for the extraterrestrial to discern these things.

Dan knew that it was now or never. "I— I want to... I need to... go back. In time, I mean."

Willie listened as the man with the dog recounted the story of Maya, and how he intended to return to a time before her devastating encounter with a stranger, prevent it from occurring, and thus invalidate her untimely death—after he successfully located Reno and Gretchen, of course.

The alien stood there rubbing his chin. He regarded Dan with a stern look. "We are not running a shuttle service, Mister Rivers. Time travel is not to be taken lightly. One person was displaced and therefore one person should return. Naturally, it should be that same person. That is the situation that will incur the least amount of upheaval to the normal balance of things--half of one, six dozen of the other, as you say. Each person has his own effect upon your world--which is usually, but not always, limited to his own circle of acquaintances. However, if hordes of individuals should begin ingressing and egressing willy-nilly through time, the effect would be multiplied. History could be changed. Quite possibly to the detriment of all. Do you understand, Mister Rivers?"

Dan's heart sank. "Yes… yes, I understand."

Willie began to turn away, as if signaling the end of their dialogue, but he turned back again and Dan thought he detected a glimmer somewhere in the deep black void of his eyes. "There are extenuating circumstances in this case, however," the alien said. "The exact whereabouts of Mister Vegas are currently unknown. If we are unsuccessful in locating him before my crew and I depart your planet, it WOULD be possible for someone such as yourself to take his place. You would be returning for the purpose of doing good, after all."

Dan looked down at Harv. "What about this little guy?"

"He is like your child, yes?"

"Yes."

"Then kids fly free!"

Dan rubbed his palm across his forehead. This was all too much. "I wonder if I might ask… Just how it's done."

You refer to time travel, Mister Rivers?"

'Yes."

Willie cocked his head, as if pondering how to go about this. "You mentioned earlier that you are a person who speaks on the radio."

"Talk show host—that's my title... or was."

"Wonderful medium, this radio. But like much of your technology, it can be used for great good, or great evil."

"Tell me about it."

"I believe, then, that one such as yourself should be able to grasp my explanation. The past, present, and future exist simultaneously--but on different FREQUENCIES."

"There's a word that's right up my alley."

"Imagine that you are slowly rotating a radio knob from left to right across the dial. You land on a particular station that is playing music. That's the present. You continue moving across the dial toward the next station on a different frequency. This new station that you are moving toward, but haven't yet reached--may be called the future. The frequency you have just moved away from is now the past. Are you with me so far, Mister Rivers?"

"Yes... well, ah... yes."

"Even though YOU'VE moved away from the previous station, that frequency still exists, just as the one you are moving toward exists, though you haven't yet experienced it. In your world, however, you can move across the dial in only one direction--toward the future. We, on the other hand, have mastered the art of rotating the knob in either direction."

"It… it makes a kind of sense—if you think of it that way. Now, technologically—how is it done? I mean, I may not be able to grasp your technical jargon and all that, but—"

"YOU may not be able to grasp it, Mister Rivers?" Willie gave a little high-pitched warbling kind of laugh. "What do you think we are-- scientists? Can you explain to me, in minute detail, how your automobile works—or do you just get in and turn the key without thinking about it? We are interplanetary businessmen of sorts… we leave that type of thing to the experts. Beyond that, however, there are certain principles your greatest minds have yet to discover. For our part, suffice it to say, we know which buttons to push."

The windmills of Dan's mind were turning at breakneck speed. Gretchen had gone to find Reno. Locate Gretchen and you'll likely turn up Reno as well. It would then be the time-displaced rocker's choice to stay or go back. Somehow, Dan would have to dissuade him from choosing the latter. How would he do it, and what if he failed?

His mind entertained a darker scenario. If necessary, would he kidnap Reno, the man he had befriended that night in the desert? Take him out of commission just long enough to make the switch? Would he? Could he?

How far would he go?

Forty-Three

It is the day after Christmas and Gretchen, Reno, and the others have returned home safely. But the issue of who will get the free pass back to the sixties has not been settled. To break the impasse, Gretchen has devised a contest of sorts. Dan and Reno are sitting side by side in high back chairs a few feet apart. Reno has summoned his loyal groupie friend, Jackie, from her feces infested trailer.

Gretchen explains the rules of the contest. "I will flip a coin. Jackie will call it in the air. If she calls it, she will get to choose between Mister Rivers and Mister Vegas., Otherwise, I choose. The men will remove their pants. At the signal, Jackie will manually stimulate her designated partner, and I will do the same with mine. The man who is able to delay his orgasm the longest will be declared the winner, and will be allowed to make the trip through time with the Greys."

Jackie calls tails. It comes up heads. It is Gretchen's pick and she chooses Reno.

Just like her, Dan mutters with disgust. Always preferring the strange salami.

He looks at Jackie. She is just as Reno had described her on the night of their camping trip—a decrepit looking hag, aged beyond her years. She is clad in a bright red University of Arizona T-shirt and a pair of flannel pajama bottoms with ducks painted on them. She smells of stale cigars and cat piss.

Dan looks at Gretchen. Your penchant for pecker will backfire this time, my dear, he says to himself. There is no way this pathetic crone will get me off before Reno pops his rocks in the presence of your exquisite beauty.

Gretchen places a CD in a boom box on the table beside him. To make the contest fair, the women will have to keep time with the beat. The song begins. It is an old one from the sixties that both Reno and Dan know well: "Everyday People" by Sly and the Family Stone. The phrase *different strokes for different folks* is repeated several times throughout the lyric. Dan has to give it to her—she IS creative.

Gretchen grips Reno's already turgid member in her hand and shouts, "GO!"

Piece of cake, Dan figures. He is totally limp and intends to stay that way. He watches as the woman he once thought he loved primes Reno's pump in her expert fashion. She looks at him, not Reno, and she sticks her tongue out in a lascivious way. His face flushes with anger and disgust. Why, she's nothing but a common whore! Why couldn't he have seen it in the beginning? And how could he have stooped so low as to participate in this kind of depravity? Well... there WAS Brigitta. He doesn't want to think about THAT on top of everything else just now.

The loathing he feels for Gretchen has delayed him from noticing that Jackie is now causing his own soldier to stand at attention. He looks down at himself. My God—what a grip! She knows exactly where to place the thumb and forefinger, and how much pressure to use. No—this can't be happening. But it is.

He tries to think of something to distract himself from the delicious sensations he's experiencing—in spite of their highly unappealing source. He looks over at Reno, who is obviously trying to hold back, though his eyes are somewhere up in the top of his head. The music plays on. Different strokes for different folks. Dan needs to concentrate on something as far removed from sensuality as possible. Aha! THE POPE! That's it. He'll think about the pope sitting there in his white robe—the symbol of purity.

Jackie's rhythmic onslaught continues. They didn't call her "Jack-off Jackie" for nothing. Yeah, she's still got it. Must be like riding a bicycle.

This is a battle of titans. The two most accomplished weenie whackers in the world matched in a head-to-head duel.

Unfortunately for Dan, things are coming to a head much too quickly--even as he has projected his mind inside the cloistered walls of the Vatican.

He doesn't want to look at Gretchen again but he feels compelled to do so. She has turned into an eerie, otherworldly creature. Two red laser beams of light shoot from her eyes. She aims the beams directly at his scrotum, sending a current through him that causes his sap to rise and geyser into the air, pasting the ceiling and hanging there in thick globulets—his moment of involuntary ecstasy kicking in even as he cries, NO! IT'S NOT FAIR… NOT FAIR!

Dan woke in a sweat, still mouthing his protest. After a moment he lay still. He blinked his eyes and looked around the room to get his bearings. What a fucked up dream.

He breathed a heavy sigh of relief. All things were still possible. That was good, on the one hand—potentially disastrous on the other.

Harv stood on the bed, giving him a quizzical look. He felt something wet farther down on the sheet, and knew that it wasn't perspiration. Jesus, he hadn't had a wet dream since he was fourteen years old. Harv started sniffing the wet spot to determine if it was something he should be lapping up.

Dan jumped up and began tearing the sheet from the bed. "Don't even think about it, buddy," he said.

Forty-Four

You could say it was "close" inside the cab of that odiferous hunk of steel—with Sondra riding Reno's lap (a familiar spot) and Gretchen sitting astride the Russian. The friction created by her bottom as the big truck bounced along the rutted dirt road leading away from… well, wherever the hell they were, triggered Sergei's involuntary response—much to his chagrin—and it was only through conscious willpower that Our Lady of the Unorthodox Sperm Bank was able to curtail her natural instinct to pet the protuberance that poked her.

While his passengers laughed and sent war whoops into the air, Billy glanced at the gas gauge and cursed under his breath. They were running on empty. He didn't want to be the one to rain on their parade, but the reality was that it was about to come to an abrupt halt.

Reno muttered something unintelligible. Sergei spat in the dirt. The women sat along the side of the ditch and surveyed the landscape. They were still a thousand miles from anywhere—or might as well be.

There were only two choices. Stay with the truck and wait for someone to come along—which didn't seem likely—or follow the road on foot and hope that it would lead them back to civilization. Before they could come to a consensus on what to do, fate played its trump card.

A plume of dust appeared down the road, moving toward them from the direction they had just traveled. As it came slowly into view, there was no mistaking the vehicle for anything but Milburn's panel truck. Thankfully, someone had the presence of mind to rip the agent's weapon from his hand back at the warehouse, and that someone was Sergei. He stepped forward now, legs spread apart in the dirt like Clint Eastwood in a spaghetti western.

This was personal.

From out of the ether (or just inside his head) came the trilling flute sound from the tune, "The Good, The Bad, And The Ugly" that he'd heard repeatedly on the local Music of Your Life station. It had been those old western movies that originally attracted him to this part of the world. Now he had stepped inside the movie. The agent had senselessly murdered his girlfriend... well, former girlfriend... okay, one time traveling companion who never did the trick with him. Didn't matter. The hurt was still there.

The fed had to pay.

Lawrence Milburn stepped from his truck and approached the group with outstretched hands—palms up—to show that he was unarmed. He was a man of many smiles, each one geared to fit the specific occasion. The smile he wore now seemed to say, *What happened dudes? We were having such a good time and then you wimped out on me!*

Sergei withdrew the gun he'd tucked down the front of his jeans. "NOW we see who is the asshole," he said.

"Hold on," said Milburn. "I come in peace. You guys didn't really think I was out to do you harm, now did you?" His eyes scanned each stern face as though he were appealing to a jury.

"I take you in to the authorities," Sergei said. "We ride in your truck."

Milburn looked down at the Russian's feet. "Very well, but you'd better watch it... your shoelace is untied."

Sergei averted his gaze for a split second, and that's all it took. No American youngster over the age of five would have fallen for the oldest trick in the book, but some dumb foreigner might. And did. The agent's lightning kick hit its mark and the weapon went flying from the Russian's fingers.

In the mad scramble that followed, Milburn came up with the gun. The smile on his face changed as he stepped back and ordered everyone to line up against the Thrifty Sanitation sign on the side of the big crap conveyance. "The balance of power has shifted, my fine red devil. Just as your country is no longer a major player in the world, YOU are no longer in control of this game."

"Nice trick you pull," Sergei said. "But now I tell you something. I take all bullets out of gun but one. One to shoot you with. At same time I am thinking, if somehow he gets gun back, he can't kill us all. Shoot one of us maybe, but then the others will tear him apart."

The agent's smile disappeared as the momentum shifted again.

Gretchen spoke. She was ready to play her ace in the hole. "You can take me if you like, but let the rest of them go. I know who you are... I know WHAT you are, and I'll tell these people right now. One of them will get word to your superiors. Once you're under suspicion, you'll never survive the scrutiny."

He stared at her for a long moment. Then he looked away, remembering not to fall under her spell. He had thought about her after he'd awoken from his ill-timed nap—thought about her as he lurched to his vehicle and retrieved the ignition keys from their hiding place. Putting two and two together as he kicked it into gear and headed out after them. Now he was sure of who SHE was, and that she'd sensed—he wasn't sure how—the truth about himself.

He almost had to laugh. Thinking that Reno Vegas was his biggest threat, when all along it had been this exotically beautiful woman. Thinking that a man who might convince the public that space aliens exist could start the snowball that would eventually bury him rolling in his own direction—when an unlikely, but more immediate danger existed in the body of this temptress. "All right, sister," he said, gathering his composure. "Let's you and me go for a ride. The rest of 'em can go to hell for all I care."

Gretchen stepped forward and Milburn took her by the arm. He held the gun on the others as the two of them backed away toward the flagship of Elmer's Exterminating.

"No, dude—take me!" Reno blurted. "I'm the one you wanted in the first place."

"It's all right... I'll be all right," Gretchen assured them, utterly clueless as they were to what had just transpired.

* * *

They headed down the road in silence. He had handcuffed her, but otherwise she was unrestrained. "I can't be exposed," he said finally, unaware of the double meaning the statement had for her. It had been the "exposure" of his member that day in her living room that revealed to her the secret he had spent his life trying to conceal. Unlike the rounded head of a human penis, a hybrid's organ was somewhat pointed at the crown. "Beyond the personal ramifications," he continued, "you must surely understand what it would mean for our kind everywhere in the world. You think you've seen or read about discrimination—the way blacks were treated prior to the civil rights movement... the Japanese internment camps during the Second World War... but you ain't seen nothing yet, sister. We'd be like lab animals—inspected, injected, and dissected."

Gretchen tasted salty tears as she said, "I've dedicated my life to a great cause—helping to create new lives. Beings like ourselves. Someday we will outnumber them and this planet will be better for it."

Her captor shook his head. "It was a mistake from the beginning. They have only tunnel vision and they are content with their simple explanations. Their Mother Goose concept of God and the universe. I have sought to deny that part of me that you glorify in yourself. I have striven to be like them—when in Rome and all that. Because they will kill us, plain and simple. They will kill us."

They fell silent again. Then, out of the blue, he began making small talk. He commented on the weather. He drew her attention to what he thought were interesting features of the landscape—as if they were a married couple from Sheboygan on a motor tour of the southwest.

"Where are you taking me?" she asked finally.

"Out of circulation," he said, without missing a beat.

Before they hit the main roads he stopped and made her lie down in the back, placing a piece of tape over her mouth. With the vehicle in motion again, he continued with his inane commentary.

Gretchen was a captive audience.

Forty-Five

Two days after Dan's initial meeting with the Greys, he and his faithful canine companion were summoned back to Cletus's cabin. They waited inside as Willie tended to something in the garage. When the extraterrestrial returned he said, "Mister Rivers, there is good news. I just sent a transmission from our craft to the leader of the gang that abducted Reno Vegas and created this pimple that he is in."

"Uh... *pickle,* I think is the word you want there."

"Ah yes—'pickle.' I will make a note of that. Anyway, I inquired as to whether they had placed an implant into the body of the earthling they unceremoniously snatched from your year of 1969. Yes, he recalled—feisty bastard too. Kicked and cursed the whole time. But as he recollected, one had indeed been inserted underneath the skin of the man's reproductive organ... standard procedure with this crew. This would allow them to track the earthling's whereabouts—and so I asked him to provide those coordinates to me.

"He got a little huffy then, but I reminded him that once we return to the mother ship, we could kick his ass in a dogfight any day. I won't go into the language he used after that, but he knows which side his butt is breaded on, so he relayed the information to me. Using something akin to your satellite imaging—but far more advanced, of course--it appears that Mister Vegas is located in a relatively uninhabited area near the settlement of Sedona. He is next to a large conveyance of some sort—larger than your automobiles—which is in a stationary position. Which means we can zip over there rather... instantaneously, by your standards."

Dan's head was spinning over this promising turn of events. "Let's blow this pop stand, then!"

"Oh, joy," said Willie. That is another one I'll have to write down." He glanced down at Harv and frowned.

"He's totally housebroken," Dan said, doing some mind reading of his own.

Forty-Six

Inside the craft (which Cletus had affectionately dubbed "Nelly Belle"), Willie looked embarrassed as he explained that the engine—to use a term an earthling could comprehend—wouldn't start.

"What do we do now?" Dan asked.

"Go and get Cletus from the cabin," Willie said, making a shooing motion with his hand. "This happened once before."

After a minute Cletus ambled out to the garage and sized up the saucer like a mechanic (which he was) giving the once over to an aging Buick. Then, without warning, he delivered a swift, engineer booted kick to the accessible underside of the craft. A soft humming noise emanated from the space vehicle and Willie gave Cletus a thumbless thumbs-up through the cockpit window.

Dan felt simultaneously exhilarated and scared shitless at the prospect of his first ride in a UFO. He looked around. Nelly Belle's interior was obviously scaled down—from the seat he was scrunched up in, to the decided lack of headroom—to accommodate a more diminutive type of passenger.

"Er... you're not concerned about tooling around in this thing in broad daylight?" he asked.

"The prospect of that doesn't knock the dirt off my dick," Willie said. Dan gave him a curious look.

"However, there is actually less chance of being detected than at night, as any airborne object is hard to identify with sunlight reflecting off its surface."

"Let's do it then."

* * *

"Gee, there wasn't even time for in-flight peanuts," Dan said.

"Look out across the field," Willie directed. "The party you seek is over there."

Dan could make out the shape of a truck in the distance and a few souls milling about. He trekked across the field where the saucer had set down to meet up with the group that he prayed included Gretchen as well as Reno.

Willie stayed with Harv inside the craft, leery of shutting its power plant down in the absence of Cletus's mechanical expertise. He dangled bite-sized dog biscuits above the canine's nose and squealed with delight when his new buddy snapped them up.

The escapees got Dan up to speed with the long-story-short of their capture and detainment; their subsequent break for freedom; and, sadly, the retaking of their beautiful comrade.

"Milburn!" Dan spat. But his ever-increasing sense of urgency to remove Gretchen from harm's way was moving toward a head on collision with his determination to supplant Reno as the Grey's sole human passenger on their retro journey through time. His argument was solid, he thought. Since the younger man already knew how the world turned out in the interim, why go back? Why not stay and live the drama like everyone else, clueless as to what lies ahead?

He looked around and saw Reno walking away, separating himself from the others—heading down the road apiece to regain his own personal space. Dan started after him, but Sondra called him back.

"There are things about Reno we haven't told you yet," she said.

"Shoot."

Sondra winced at his choice of words. "There was a young woman... his traveling companion. Her name was Alicia. She... was murdered by agent Milburn."

"What?"

"Gunned down before he took the rest of us prisoner. Reno's still taking it pretty hard."

Dan was stunned by this bizarre development. It took a moment for his brain to compute what it meant. And then it hit him like a rotten tomato upside the head, dribbling down in tiny seeds of meaning.

Dan and Maya. Reno and Alicia.

"There's something else you should know," Sondra continued.

On the surface, she looked to Dan like an older chick with spectacular jugs who knew they were her best feature—who knew they were the reason why men, even younger ones, would still show some interest in her—and yet, at this moment, studying the worry lines that grooved her face like the canals of Mars beneath that flaming red mop, there was a Mother Teresa-ness about her. A heartfelt concern for the weary time-traveler that transcended tits in the greater scheme of things.

"Reno is aging," she said. "Not like you and me... he's aging prematurely. Faster everyday—like a rider on a centrifuge."

"You mean, he's going to be old before his time?"

"In a heartbeat, relatively speaking. But that won't matter as long as he makes it back to where he came from."

Dan turned away from her. He could see Reno still a good distance down the road, but walking back towards them now. He moved slowly in that direction, gathering his thoughts. The two of them would meet somewhere in the middle and have their moment.

Golden images of Maya streamed through his mind like a music video with a bittersweet soundtrack. That first bright day on the beach. A candle flame dancing between them, softly illuminating their faces as they held each other's gaze. Passions ignited… and angry words that threatened to extinguish the flame.

Something fluttered past him—or he imagined it did.

A butterfly.

He flashed back to the ethical dilemma Gretchen had presented to him in their initial conversation, a thousand million years ago.

He had been a fool. You're dealt one hand. You play it, and live with the results. Move too slow and the window of opportunity sprouts a sign that says *Out To Lunch.* Then you wait and you wait for the next one to open, and the best you can hope for is that you've learned something from the pain—something that may help you to do better somewhere down the line.

Reno *belonged* back in '69, but due to some twisted quirk of fate, HIS opportunity—to fly or crash and burn—had been snatched away.

Dan's chance—and all that mattered now—was to save the only other woman he'd ever really cared about.

They were close enough now to make out each other's faces. (Did Reno's pinky finger just exit his nasal cavity?) No matter. The younger man smiled in recognition. They stopped two feet apart. A raven passed overhead, its caw floating on the wind. They sealed the deal in a silent bear-hug embrace.

Forty-Seven

Reno and his not so long lost friend Sondra, along with the Russian (who was all agog at the prospect of joy riding in a real live UFO), accepted Willie's offer of protective custody with Cletus and the Greys--until the moment when they would be ready to transport the man ahead of his time back to where he came from. But there was work to be done now. Willie would no more allow Gretchen, of whom he was quite fond, to come to a bad end than would Dan. Having dropped the others off at the cabin, he and part of his crew navigated Nelly Belle back to the deserted spot where Dan, Harv, and Billy had opted to stay with the truck. He gave Billy a mild telepathic brain sedative so that the ayatollah of crapola would not freak out at the sight of him.

Now, it was time for action. Willie vetoed the idea of going after the crazed federal agent in the saucer, especially if Milburn were hurtling down any of the main roads, which he would have to do eventually to get out of the area. Willie didn't want another Roswell—which, by the way, he told Dan, WAS an actual crash of an extra-terrestrial craft back in the forties. He punctuated his remarks with the phrase, 'Weather balloon my arse!"

That aside, they'd have to use what was at their disposal--so to speak--and that meant the big hunk of crap hauling steel and glass. Billy, of course, would captain his ship, and he was all for going after the bastard—secretly hoping to get another glimpse of the captive goddess in the process.

There was never a question of Dan's role in the mission. He could have opted to leave Harv The Wonder Dog with Cletus, but no— they were in this thing together now—inseparable come hell or high water.

There was still the problem of the empty gas tank. Wait a while, is what Willie said. He sensed that something was in the wind. Presently, another plume of dust appeared down the road—this one thinner than the maelstrom Milburn's approaching panel truck had stirred up. The distinctive revving sound of the motor identified it as a dirt bike.

It was time for Willie to do his stuff.

He stepped into the middle of the road as the rider approached. The alien cut a diminutive, yet commanding figure, as he raised his hand like a traffic cop.

The cyclist slammed on his brakes. The rear end of the bike fishtailed as its operator nearly took a tumble. The rider cursed, took his first look at Willie and said, "What the—"

Their eyes locked. The wayfarer was transfixed. The E.T. had poured something into the guy—who wasn't much more than a kid, really—poured something like wet concrete into his mind to lay the foundation for what Willie would have him do. "Are the instructions clear?" he said to the hapless stranger.

"Yes… instructions clear." The kid restarted his bike, moving like a zombie. He revved the engine and disappeared down the road.

Willie turned to Dan and Billy and said, "This earthling will be back in a short while with enough gasoline to get us to what you call a filling station. Afterward, he will not remember this encounter."

The big truck rumbled up I-17—heading north. They had come off the dirt section of what was known as the Beaver Creek Backroads Loop. When they hooked up with pavement again it was just blind reckoning that steered them this way—hoping that Milburn was moving in the same direction.

Willie whipped out his "cell" phone. It didn't look like any device Dan had ever seen. It was purple and green and gold and it had all the bells and whistles. He spoke into it for a few moments, then explained that telepathy was not one hundred percent foolproof, and that when accuracy was of the utmost importance, the Greys would reach out and touch someone in the same manner as humans. Willie had phoned his crewmembers in Nelly Belle, hovering high in the sky, waiting for further directions. He told them to scan the main arteries—at a prudent distance, of course—to see if they could spot a vehicle of the description Billy had provided.

In his lap, Willie cradled the riding helmet that had previously belonged to the hypnotized dirt biker. It was a nice one, with a mask in front shaded dark enough to conceal his appearance. With the helmet affixed to his head, and the riding gloves he'd also "borrowed" from the hapless traveler, he was just another ten-year old in a jumpsuit.

The elderly couple that had tucked in behind them in their Taurus didn't notice anything at first. They were returning home from a family reunion in Flagstaff and drove along numbly, each daydreaming about home and their comfy adjustable bed. Then the woman turned to her husband and said, "Look, George... that's the same plate number as that missing garbage truck that's been on the news... I'm sure of it!"

George and his wife didn't cotton to cell phones, being that they were retired and didn't make business calls—nor did they have teenage friends to whom they would babble mindlessly for hour upon hour. So they pulled off the highway at the next exit and made two calls from the nearest gas station. One call was to the Highway Patrol. The other was to the Phoenix radio station they relied upon for their news.

Willie answered his phone. "Uh huh," he said. "Uh huh. Uh huh. Uh huh."

Milburn's vehicle was on the same road heading north. "Step on it kid," he said to Billy. "Put the metal through the pedal!"

Billy gritted his teeth. "I've never winded 'er out, but we'll find out what she's made of." Tasting the freedom of the open road, there was some vague awareness in his mind that his bosses and family must be looking for him. He had no idea that he was a celebrity—nor was Dan, distracted and incommunicado as he'd been lately—aware of the story of the AWOL sanitation worker that had captured the nation's fancy.

The first radio bulletin about an unconfirmed sighting of the missing truck was picked up by several motorists traveling I-17. At the same time, multiple units of the Highway Patrol were speeding to intercept the vehicle.

A car full of teenagers pulled in behind the big trash transport, waving and honking their horn.

"Damn kids," Billy muttered.

A Corvette pulled alongside, then zoomed in front of them and slowed to about forty. Another vehicle pulled even, the driver straining to get a look at the occupants of the truck. Cars, pickups, and motorcycles joined the pursuit as word continued to spread. Both northbound lanes were now jammed, preventing the Highway Patrol vehicles--sirens blaring and lights flashing—from making any headway. It was a party. It was a convoy.

And Milburn was getting away.

Forty-Eight

Willie, Billie, and Dan heard the police helicopter hovering above. Harv barked excitedly. Billy glanced at the speedometer. The convoy was slowing incrementally—down to thirty-five miles per hour. Someone in front wanted to bring this little parade to a halt to see who was in possession of the re-materialized shit wagon. Someone, perhaps, wanted to be a hero. Thirty. Twenty-five. Fifteen. The big truck stopped right there on the highway along with about forty tag-along vehicles. Motorists traveling in the opposite direction slowed to a crawl and rubbernecked at the scene. Both lanes of the freeway were now effectively blocked.

The DPS officers tailing the convoy abandoned their cruisers and headed toward the truck, jogging between vehicles with guns drawn. Simultaneously, three good ol' boys from the front of the caravan hopped out of their pickup (with the gun rack in the back and the bumper sticker that read: *Keep Honking—I'm Reloading*) and advanced upon the idling stink schooner wielding baseball bats and tire irons.

Billy observed the men approaching and said, "JEE-ZUS!" Then he looked in his side mirror and saw the officers wending their way through the maze of vehicles and said, MAMA!"

The rednecks were going to get there first.

Billy looked at Willie. "Wh— what're we gonna do now?"

"Get out and come around to this side. Someone needs to help me down."

Billy opened the passenger door and lifted the diminutive extraterrestrial to the pavement.

The good ol' boys stopped short when they saw him. "Hey son," one of them said, "did these bastards kidnap you?"

A waif-like figure in his jumpsuit, helmet, and riding gloves, Willie shook his head slowly.

"That's all right son—don't be afraid," said the man. An American flag was depicted on his T-shirt. It ballooned out at the bottom where his gut hung over his belt like a gigantic teardrop about to fall. He slapped the end of a bat against his palm. "You better come with us while we take care of these here PREVERTS."

Willie lifted the helmet and made eye contact with the redneck, who had only a split second to gasp before he succumbed. He shot stares at the other two men—their mouths agape—in quick succession.

The one who'd displayed such bravado a moment ago placed the small end of the bat between his legs and began to wave it up and down and from side to side as if it were an erect penis—an enormous "woodie" as it were. His face displayed a vacant hypnotic grin. He strutted bowlegged up to a carload of teenage girls who were cackling at his antics. They squealed in feigned terror, scrambling to roll up the windows and lock their doors.

The man's companions were putting on a show of their own. Each had squatted by the side of the road—acting out the scene Willie had given them—which was to pretend they were each having a difficult bowel movement. They grunted loudly. They stuck out their tongues and made disgusting farting noises. People in nearby vehicles looked on in revulsion.

Inside the truck, Dan struggled to hold onto Harv, who wanted to leap out the window and bite them on their backsides.

The first impression the state troopers had when they arrived upon the scene was that the world had gone mad. They glanced at Willie and immediately joined the ranks of his automatons. The officers whirled in the direction of the nearest vehicle, where a young black man was stationed behind the wheel. They yanked open the driver's door, extracted the startled soul and shoved him down onto the pavement. The troopers drew their truncheons and began flailing away at the man, who was on his knees, protesting vociferously, arms raised above his head for protection. More patrolmen arrived and joined in the whomp fest.

Willie told Billy to lift him back into the cab of the truck. "Let's blow this pop stand," he said, getting the phrasing right for once.

Dan gazed back upon the violent scene. "Jesus, Willie," he said. "You've probably never heard of Rodney King, but this could set race relations in this country back forty years."

"We make no distinction among skin tones or other trivialities the way you do," the alien said calmly. "And those uniformed individuals are merely pretending to strike the man, albeit in a highly convincing way."

Billy set his jaw and gripped the steering wheel. He surveyed the logjam ahead of them.

 "Plow through them sons o' bitches," Willie exhorted.

The captain of the SS Shit Wagon grimaced. His head fell to his chest. "No," he said. "I'm done. I'd like to help you guys, but we'd never make it. This ol' truck's got a bulls-eye on her. I'll go back there and turn myself in. All the hullabaloo you've set in motion, Mister Willie, should distract everyone long enough for you all to disappear into the crowd."

Dan reached over and clasped Billy's hand. "We'll be there to back you up when this thing is over." He turned to Willie and said, "Are you familiar with the term hitch-hiking?"

"Yes," Willie replied. "But it won't be that difficult."

Billy climbed down from the truck. His name and photo had been a mainstay of the network news for days, and a cheer of recognition arose from the crowd as it closed around him. Hoisted upon shoulders, he took the hero's ride as the assemblage chanted Bill-EEE! Bill-EEE!

Dan, Willie, and Harv the Wonder Dog slipped away unnoticed.

Forty-Nine

Lawrence Milburn decided that whatever way he was going to dispose of his cargo—the one source that could effectively bring his life to an end—it needed to be sooner rather than later. But he was a male, after all, and his base instincts needed to be fed. What a waste it would be, at any rate, to put such a stunning creature down without once indulging in her charms.

The Pine Shadows Lodge had presented itself, broadcasting a kind of psychic siren song he picked up inside his head. It was a rustic country inn along route 89A between Sedona and Flagstaff, set back from the road in a secluded spot at the base of a heavily wooded hillside.

Inside the room, a burning log popped and crackled in the fireplace. Things were heating up. Gretchen lay spread-eagled on the bed, wrists and ankles lashed to the bedposts—her mouth still sealed with the strip of duct tape. Her naked body glistened with a light sheen of perspiration. She'd put on a brave face, to this point, but now the fear was spreading through her like wine spill on a carpet.

Milburn, knowing what he must ultimately do, figured that if one could die of pleasure—or at least check out immediately AFTER experiencing pleasure—well, it would be the least he could do.

Playing it by ear, he pulled open the top drawer of the bureau next to the bed. Gideon, as expected, had left his Bible. In the second drawer, much to his delight, he discovered a Jolly Green Giant sized vibrator. The apparatus was longer and thicker than most normal women might be expected to accommodate—more novelty coffee table piece than practical power tool, perhaps, but it was true to life in every other aspect, right down to the raised "veins" running along its shaft. Whoever left it behind was not the tidy sort, as the purple helmeted poontang poker still had a few dark hairs clinging to it. 'YECCHHH!"

He took it into the bathroom and gave it a thorough cleaning in the sink. He had his standards, after all. When he brought it back to the bed, Gretchen's eyes grew wide. Milburn appraised her body from head to toe. The breasts, though flatter now, were still perfectly rounded as she lay there on her back—the nipples inadvertently hard again—her pink pudendum splayed before him, inviting intrusion.

Lawrence Milburn had never experienced what could be called a normal sex life—self-conscious as he was about his "winky." He'd spurned his own kind—those who might have accepted him—to keep his identity a secret. In his relations with human females, he'd adopted the role of pleaser, so as not to focus undue attention on his aberrant appendage. He'd turned foreplay into an art. So he wasn't thinking about mounting this exquisite creature. Instead, he would utilize his new toy.

He located the on/off switch and moved it with his thumb. The device sprang to life with the sound of a thousand angry bees. "BATTERIES INCLUDED!" he shouted in triumph.

Gretchen's eyes burned him with contempt. What kind of a monster was he?

She was about to find out.

Milburn parted the labia with his fingers and found her Little Red Riding Clit hiding beneath its hood. He placed the droning dildo head gently against the suddenly exposed and vulnerable knurl. Slowly adding pressure, he rotated the head of the rubbery reproductive organ in a circular pattern, alternating with a side to side and an up and down motion.

Gretchen emitted a gasp of surprise. The vibratory power of this device was second to none.

He reached over and pulled the tape partially away from her mouth. If she screamed, he could immediately smooth it back into place, but now he wanted to hear her reaction, for that was half the fun.

Now she understood the depths of his depravity. He intended to get her off! But why? As a humiliation, no doubt. Exerting the ultimate power and control—and there was nothing she could do about it.

Milburn couldn't have known that she was multi-orgasmic. Her estranged lover had brought that out, and once you got her started... well... it was better not to think about it. She had no intention of boarding that runaway train. She would resist the mere physical machinations of a madman. They would have zero effect upon her. After all, there had to be some emotions involved, didn't there? The orgasm was not a mere physical response that could be conjured up at will whenever the snake charmer toots his flute. Even men, those patently sexual creatures, needed some dirty pictures or... the helping hand of an attractive woman.

She looked at Milburn's eyes. They were cold. Focused upon the task at hand. He was nothing like her, despite their common lineage. Despite... oh... something was building down there—but she would have none of it. She would concentrate on how thoroughly this man disgusted her. He could never produce the desired response. She would win the battle of wills.

Her first encounter with Dan flashed in her mind—the way she'd expected him to perform—and what's more, to like it. To be a machine.

Oh God—she WAS like Milburn.

But no, that was in the past—a distant and disgraceful memory. Since then her human traits had blossomed, whereas Lawrence Milburn's cold and clinical alien side had won out. Now, as she observed this

Doctor Mengele of the dildo at work, her feelings softened and she saw him as an unevolved version of herself, and she began to feel COMPASSION (something akin to what she'd felt for the rat). And as she was warmed by this unexpected emotion, as the whining ding dong did its work, she felt herself melting in that heretofore private but now shamelessly exposed place—climbing that mountain, moving inexorably toward the summit… teetering on the brink for a moment… finally crossing over into the severe-tire-damage-do-not-back-up point of no return until there was no longer any why or wherefore—the orgasm taking on a life of its own, not to be denied. Yes, she was coming against her will, and in spite of (but perhaps because of) this crossing into forbidden territory, her climax was especially strong and enduring--and sweet, like what a foodaholic who's trying to do the right thing might feel upon being force fed a Twinkie.

* * *

Entering the throes of her seventh blinding orgasm, Gretchen barely had time to catch her breath. She was a Top 40 radio station where the hits just keep on coming. Milburn knew just how to manipulate her hot button; that comprehensive compilation of nerve endings pumping out chorus after chorus of "Good Vibrations" in perfect harmony. "SHIT! FUCK! GERONIMO!" she cried, as another wave swept over her.

Then she felt the pressure from the vibrator ease off a bit and eventually cease altogether. She looked down and saw that her captor's eyes were closing as his expression shifted from the deranged intensity of a mad scientist to the sagging stupor of the delirious drunk. His body toppled like a totem pole in a strong wind and fell onto its side. He was out cold again, lying in a lump like yesterday's oatmeal, the dildo still clutched in his fingers—still whirring and purring away.

Gretchen discerned that with all the writhing she'd done during her orgasmic frenzy, the bonds that shackled her left hand to the bedpost had loosened. Realizing that it was now or never, she made a fist and jerked her wrist from side to side. The rope came loose and she slipped her hand free. The phone was just within reach on the bureau beside the bed. She maneuvered the receiver from its cradle. Looking askew at the bank of numbers, she punched in the series of digits that still held a place in her mind and in her heart. When nothing happened she remembered that you normally had to dial a 9 to get an outside line in these places. And so, with an eye on the comatose (but for how long?) pervert at her feet, she began the process anew.

Inside a well-maintained '73 Caddie, Dan Rivers' phone came to life.

"Dang, I think my ears are ringin' again," said the old gal behind the wheel.

Earlier, Willie had tapped on her window, and as she made eye contact the woman, whose name was Myrtle, had been instantly hypnotized into believing that Dan was her son, Willie her grandson, and Harv—in mischievous Willie style—her cat.

Dan picked up the phone. From what sounded like a world away, Gretchen's voice. "Dan, I need you. I— I'm so sorry about everything… that we couldn't-"

"Forget about that," he said. "Where are you?"

"I'm not sure. It's a motor lodge. Wait… there's a placard on the bureau here."

He listened as she fumbled with the card.

"It's the Pine Shadows Lodge… on 89A it says here… a secluded spot between Sedona and Flagstaff. There's nothing else around, apparently, except trees, but I'll give you the address…"

"Where's Milburn?" Dan demanded, as he scrawled the numbers on a notepad.

"He's asleep... for now."

"What's that buzzing sound?"

"Uh... it's the air conditioner. I mean the heater. It's making a racket."

"Hold on—we're on our way!"

"Dan... I love—"

He pressed the kill button on the phone, pretending he hadn't caught that last snippet.

Willie looked at the address Dan had written down. "We will find that easily," he said. "It is one of my special abilities... turn left here, Grandma."

And the radio played that forgotten song, "Radar Love."

Fifty

Keenly aware that her time was limited, Gretchen tugged on the knot
that shackled her other wrist to the opposite side bedpost and
loosened it enough to disengage the arm. She worked on the bonds
that had immobilized her legs during the terrible ordeal (well, yes—
except for those protracted moments of shameful ecstasy) and pulled
herself free. She swung her right leg over Milburn' s dead weight. All
that was needed now was to follow suit with the left and make a
break for the door. Her deliciously naked bottom momentarily
hovered over his face, which displayed an angelic slumbering smile.
She raised her leg slowly, so as not to make a sound. Slowly...
slowly... TOO LATE!

Milburn woke with a start—the horror flick monster springing
inevitably back to life. He seized her thighs in his cruel and powerful
grip and pulled her toward him until—to her shock and surprise—she
was straddled atop his suddenly reanimated face! Reflexively, his
tongue slipped inside her crevasse and began to lap at its sweet juices.

Squealing and squirming, she tried to break free, which only served to
slaver her essence over a wider area of his face. "BASTARD!" she
cried. "ABOMINATION! EMBODIMENT OF ALL THE EVIL IN
THE UNIVERSE!"

There was only one way out of this sticky situation. Facing Milburn's
lower half, she brought her fist down hard and delivered an on target
hammer strike to his groin. Men are men—even with a partially
transmundane lineage—and the sheer agony spreading northward
from his southern region redirected his priorities instantaneously. He
released his grip and doubled up with the pain as she bolted for the
door: She fumbled with the chain lock, hands trembling, making the
task of getting out of the room more difficult than it ordinarily would

be. At last, with the lock undone (and it would only take a second, she thought), Gretchen tried to scoop up one or two articles of her clothing that were scattered about the floor.

Partially recovered from the pain, Milburn sprang into action. His jacket was draped over a chair and there was something in its pocket that would put an end to this little uprising. He removed the hypodermic needle—the same device he'd used to knock her out prior to lugging her over his shoulders like a sack of potatoes from his vehicle to their quarters. He leaped across the room and plunged the needle into her buttocks just as the doorknob was turning in her hand. She slumped to the floor as the world turned black again.

"Make a left here, Grandma," Willie said. "Our destination is at the end of this dirt road."

The old gal had just negotiated the turn when flashing red lights appeared in her rearview mirror. She pulled slowly to the shoulder.

"Ma'am, you did not employ your turn signal back there," said the helmeted motorcycle cop in a deadly serious tone as he positioned his head to peer inside the car.

"Oh, my..." said Myrtle, fishing around inside her purse for the mandatory license and registration.

"Grrrrr," said Harvey from the back seat.

Dan grimaced and stared straight ahead. A déjà vu feeling of helplessness poured over him. It's happening AGAIN, his mind told him. *Too late... going to be... too late.*

"That your grandchild, ma'am?" asked the cop, eyeing Willie in his helmet.

"Yes—such a fine boy," said Myrtle.

"You like motorcycles, son?" said the pain-in-the-ass, his tone softening.

Willie remained motionless and silent.

Dan observed him out of the corner of his eye. What's wrong? he wanted to shout. Trance this guy!

No response.

The cop's mood turned sour again. "Going to have to issue you a ticket, ma'am."

"Fuck!" said Dan under his breath.

"What was that, sir?"

"Uh... I was just saying darn the luck."

Gretchen came slowly to. Head on her chest, the first thing she saw was her nakedness. But she was no longer inside the room. Still groggy, she checked out her surroundings. Tall conifers enveloped her. Trying to move, she realized that she was bound to one of them. A corner of the motel edifice was dimly visible through the forest— far enough away that a scream would likely fall on deaf ears.

The sun would soon be descending, merging into the hills. She began to shiver. Her nipples jutted like two miniature erections.

Then, the sound of someone tramping through the underbrush. Milburn appeared with an armload of firewood. He dropped the loose branches and larger twigs he'd collected at her feet. Squatting, he arranged the kindling in a circle around the tree.

Stung by the realization of what was about to happen, Gretchen cried out. "No! Oh please, no! Not this way!" She struggled against her bonds but the rope held fast. "I'll do... ANYTHING."

So there it was--the final bid of the hopelessly doomed. He looked up. "You've already done what I intended fer ye—WHORE! Back there on yonder bed." (Why had he suddenly developed a Scottish accent?). "Had ye resisted, I might have spared thee."

"Oh... my God," she moaned, tears streaming down her cheeks, head falling to her chest once more.

The caddy screeched to a halt in front of the Pine Shadows Lodge. Dan, Willie, and Harv piled out and hit the ground running.

"Don't forget to eat your vegetables, boys," Myrtle called after them.

The sulking gendarme had taken his sweet time to write the ticket, and when they were moving again, Willie explained that he'd felt his hypnotic abilities waning—like a battery losing its charge—from zonking so many earthlings in such a short time span. By choosing not to zap the cop as well—and in the process costing them valuable time—he was rolling the dice, hoping to conserve his powers for a possible confrontation with Gretchen's abductor. It was a judgment call. "I can't tune in to where she is right now," he said. "Just begin knocking on doors."

Dan dispensed with the idea of knocking, turning each knob instead and shouldering his weight into the doors in hopes they might give way. It was in this manner that he burst into the room—stumbled, really, nearly kissing the floor.

He saw the giant dildo—still whirring away on top of the bed.

"Aaaghh... Aaaghh!" He reeled back in shock and disgust. He thought he might toss his cookies. Among the articles of clothing scattered about the floor, he recognized a T-shirt as one that belonged to Gretchen.

Conjuring unspeakable debauchery, he staggered from the room in search of Willie. It was then that he heard the plaintive cry—a sorrowful wail, really. The sound, though somewhat distant and faint, was unmistakable.

Gretchen was calling his name.

He met Willie coming around the corner of the building. Without a word, they plunged into the woods behind the lodge. With Harv leading the way, the three of them crashed through the trees and underbrush, honing in on the sound of her voice. After a while, the wailing ceased, and there was only the dog's panting, the rustle of the wind, and the sound of twigs crunching beneath their feet.

Harv's sniffer was right on, as at last they arrived upon the scene of Gretchen's horror and debasement. They found Milburn in a crouch, attempting to ignite the kindling with a cigarette lighter.

Dan gasped as he took it all in: The coarse rope cutting into the tormented beauty's milky skin as she strained against her bonds; the strip of duct tape muffling her cries—the eyes wild and pleading as they met his.

Milburn turned, then stood to face the intruders. He drew the .357 Magnum from his waistband. "Somehow, I knew it would come down to you and me, Rivers. I sensed it that first day back at the station." He regarded Dan's companions with a smirk. "A kid and a stupid mutt? Really... I suppose Norman Rockwell is going to step out from behind a tree and paint me out of the picture now."

Harv growled.

It was an odd little assemblage, to be sure, with four species—human, alien, hybrid, and canine represented—though the crazed G-man wasn't hip to that fact, as his numbers, had he thought about it, would have added up to only three.

Milburn motioned toward his captive. "Behold the WHORE! Behold the WITCH! The proscribed punishment for witchery is death by fire!"

"Give it up, Milburn," Dan said. "I just called the local authorities on my cell—you're as good as nailed right now. Don't make it worse on yourself." He was gambling that it was a good enough bluff to turn the situation around.

Oblivious, Gretchen's tormentor produced a can of lighter fluid from his hip pocket. "Damn kindling seems to be a mite damp. Better soak it with this stuff."

"Do it NOW," Dan whispered to Willie. "Take this guy out. Make him think that gun is so hot he can't hold onto it."

"I've already tried," the alien said sheepishly. "My... uh, battery is still low... nothing's working."

Like a professor preparing his demonstration, Milburn gingerly stepped around the tree and stood at Gretchen's side. His eyes beamed with deranged delight. He dribbled some of the lighter fluid into her pubic hair. The volatile liquid beaded up and glistened like raindrops on a newly shined pair of shoes.

She looked on in helpless horror.

Milburn began to sing in a terrible falsetto voice. "Someone left the fur pie in the rain... doo doo doo doo doo ... can't take it... took so long... to bake it..." He flicked his Bic and a flame shot from its top. "You want hot pussy, Rivers? I'll give you hot pussy!"

As the frenzied fed bent down to apply the flame to the naked beauty's mound, Dan saw his brief window of opportunity open, as it has for countless individuals through the ages, only to slam shut on their turkey necks when they poked their heads through.

He who hesitates is fucked.

Head down, he barreled forward. It had been a long time—back to his high school football days (spent primarily warming the bench)—since he'd attempted a flying tackle, but his trajectory was true and he slammed into the aberrant agent knee high. Blindsided, Milburn buckled and toppled backward, fumbling the can of lighter fluid from one hand, but maintaining possession of the firearm in the other. Dan pounced on him and straddled his chest. He socked him hard in the kisser.

Harv The Wonder Dog joined the fray—clamping his jaws down onto Milburn's left ear, snarling and shaking his head from side to side—the lobe a piece of raw meat lodged in the canine's grip.

Milbum snarled back, and for a moment he looked every bit the otherworldly creature—more bestial than human, though Dan was still clueless as to the truth of that.

Tapping into an adrenalin fueled reserve of strength, the hybrid head case wrenched free of his adversaries and struggled to his feet, though a chunk of his ear remained inside the dog's mouth.

Harv gummed the flesh tentatively with a kind of grimace, then spat it out.

Milburn, still clutching the gun, trained the weapon nervously on Dan... then Harv... then back on Dan again.

Gretchen looked on helplessly, hoping against hope that her captor might nod off again.

But it was not to be.

"Turned the tables on you turdsuckers again," Milburn said, gulping air. "When are you going to learn?" He took a step toward Dan, now on his knees, and placed the gun barrel against his forehead. (The man who held the cards took little notice of the child-like figure facing away from him and bending over, seemingly fascinated by something in the dirt.)

Dan looked up into his adversary's eyes to show that he was not afraid. And it was more than false bravado, as a feeling of serenity washed over him, and he knew that whatever was about to come down, wherever he would be in a few seconds—still on this earth or hurtling into another dimension—it was part of a design that was bigger than all of them. And it was all right.

A sharp crack, like that of a gunshot, reverberated through the trees and set the birds a twitter. In that horrifying instant, Gretchen expected to be watching the love of her life die. Instead, agent Milburn, his mouth fallen open and the maniacal expression frozen on his face, slumped to the ground—the weapon tumbling from his hand.

Fifty-One

Mister Milburn was tied up and couldn't answer the phone. He was slumped in a hardback motel chair--extremities bound with the same cruel cord that only minutes ago had constrained his beautiful sex slave. The man's dazed expression signified that he still didn't know what hit him.

Inside her duds again (at long last), Gretchen engaged her lover in a fierce embrace---clinging to him even as he responded to the imploring phone.

Dan had just said to Willie, "I still can't believe you cold cocked this guy by shooting a laser beam out of your BUTT! What verve! What imagination! What an aim!"

Willie pooh-poohed the act with a wave of his hand. "We were lucky my powers returned when they did. Our race is capable of many things, though such measures are normally reserved for dire emergencies. Speaking of emergencies..." He made a beeline for the bathroom and slammed the door.

Dan lifted the receiver and spoke to the Flagstaff police detective who was returning his call. He'd seen those movies where the local fuzz would butt heads with the feds, and it was no love fest on either side. If there were any truth to that, the locals were going to have a field day with this rotten apple; however, to protect Gretchen and the rest of her kind, there would be no mention of Milburn's little secret. On that point, ironically, Dan and his adversary would agree--the world was ill prepared for it.

Dan jotted an address and some directions onto his note pad as he spoke to the detective. He wanted to deliver his package directly to the police station. That would give Willie's crew enough time to locate their leader and whisk him back to Cletus's place.

And so, as the camera pulls back, we see agent M. all wrapped up in himself—bearing an uncanny resemblance to Jack Nicholson in the snowdrift in the closing scene of *The Shining*.

Fifty-Two

From her office down the hail, Stacy heard the ruckus out in the reception area. Instinctively, she knew that Bruno was back. It had only been a few weeks since his last Java slinging spree. A few weeks since she'd taken up with Mike Fallon, relegating Bruno to the role of shunned suitor—but it had seemed like ages.

Fallon was now dipping his wick into the new receptacle... er, receptionist. Stacy knew it, even as he continued to profess his allegiance to her. All the little signs were there. Fewer dinner dates. Fewer bedroom dates. He attributed the drop off to home maintenance. Gotta throw one into the old lady every now and then to keep the peace. Stacy understood that was a given when you carry on with a married man. But now, whenever she saw him, she wanted to ask—in the most sarcastic kind of way—if he wasn't spreading himself a little thin amongst the three of them.

Bruno was yelling now. Stacy had underestimated the depth of his feelings. She edged her way down the hall until she could see a slice of the reception area while remaining tucked away from view.

"I wanna see her!" Bruno shouted. He had a baby face with a shock of curly black hair falling into his dark frenetic eyes. He had no neck. His arm was outstretched in a menacing manner. A jar of some unidentified liquid was in his hand.

Candy, the receptionist, had been given standing orders to eighty-six any male callers asking for Stacy. Tell them she moved to Borneo. Whatever.

Bruno got louder. "Don't give me that shit—I SAID I wanna see Stacy!"

Candy held her ground.

Kirshbaum heard the commotion and came out of his office.

Bruno uncapped the bottle, and with a wide back and forth slashing motion—reminiscent of Zorro carving his initial into some villain's chest—he began to sling the liquid onto desk, wall, receptionist, General Manager.

"Ooh, ick!" said Candy.

"Fuck!" said Kirshbaum.

Bruno was just hitting his stride. He spun round like an Olympic shot putter, splattering the remaining walls, plants, and the control room window.

Timing is everything, and right on cue Mike Fallon pushed his head through the main door. Before he could emit a roar, which was what he would have done, the last of the jar's contents caught him full in the face. He stood there—incredulous, horror stricken, unable to comprehend the scene.

Kirshbaum struggled to remove his shirt. "This smells like… like…"

"It smells like PISS," said Stacy, announcing her presence. "That's because it IS. He works at a drug testing lab."

"Sta-CEE," Bruno blubbered. "I just wanted to talk to you."

Fallon sneered at his henchman. "Get the sonofabitch," he ordered.

The GM sized up the urine slinger and turned to Candy. "Call 911," he said.

Bruno bolted for the door and was out into the parking lot before anyone actually moved.

Fallon made no attempt to stop him. He won't get away," he said smugly. He looked at the new receptionist, who was clutching the phone receiver but had not yet dialed. "What's the matter with you? Make the call."

Stacy looked at Fallon and saw him, really saw him for the first time—the stars in her eyes rapidly dissolving into streaking meteors burning themselves out over the desert. At the same time she saw in Bruno a simple and pure (though somewhat impulsive) soul.

She shot Candy one of those icy looks that only one woman can give to another. "DON'T make the call," she said.

Stacy trained her gaze upon the owner of KSUK radio. "Not unless Mister Fallon's wife wants to hear about his escapades with at least two of his female employees—meaning myself and Miz Bimbo over here."

Fallon's pie hole dropped open wide enough (well, nearly) to stuff his ego into it. Candy flashed him an indignant look and unceremoniously dropped the receiver back into its cradle.

Stacy heard her estranged beau's Chevy revving up outside. She pushed past Fallon and was out the door before he could speak. "Bruno!" she cried. "I'm coming, Bruno!"

The stranger rode into town. He was traveling light—just a duffel bag with a few essentials (and a few more in the trunk of his car), for he was not planning to stay long. He drove around looking for a watering hole where he could kill some time before setting his plan into motion.

690 KSUK was playing on the car radio. He listened with bemused interest, as he had since he'd drawn close enough to Tucson to pick up the signal. Now, the brief golden glow of twilight signaled that it would soon be time to go to work.

It was New Year's eve—1999.

Fifty-Three

Dan looked at his watch. Willie had been holed up in the crapper for twenty minutes and there was no sign he'd emerge any time soon.

"Keep an eye on our friend here," he told Gretchen. "Nature calls… we're stepping out into the woods for a moment."

No problem, she thought. The guy's wrapped up in a neat little package—all he needs is a pretty bow on his head.

But Dan had never been a Boy Scout, and his artistry with the rope was nothing special—no sheepshanks or fancy stuff like that--and though he'd lashed the prisoner's arms behind his back, he had also fashioned the knots back there as well, unwittingly leaving them in close proximity to the man's fingers. And so, while pretending to be zonked and incoherent, agent Milburn furtively worked on the accessible clumps.

Gretchen closed her eyes to give them a moment's rest. Dan and Harv would be back in a minute or two. She had been through a freakish experience. Her mind went to work with that thought, and the lyrics to "It's A Most Unusual Day" began running through her head. A catchy little ditty. And though songs have rhyme, they have no reason, and will lodge inside your brain, appropriate or not to the occasion.

Outside the inn, Dan found that he needed to traipse a good ways into the woods to avoid the possible indelicacy of being observed draining his crankcase. He unzipped his fly. Harv lifted his leg.

Inside the room, Gretchen's eyes fluttered open to a Kruegeresque nightmare.

Milburn stood over her, gazing down with his sick sardonic smile.

"How—" The words choked in her throat.

He lassoed her with a length of rope and immediately squeezed it tight enough around her neck to let her know he meant business. "Don't scream," he said. "Or I'll choke the life out of you right here." He grabbed her roughly by the arm. "Let's go, sister!"

With Willie still tending to his business in the bathroom, and Dan following suit in the woods, Milburn had a clear path to freedom.

He pushed her out the door. The sun had all but crapped out for the day, with only the last vestiges of twilight standing between the dark and the light. He forced his once—and again captive to struggle to the top of the hill adjacent to the inn. Maintaining the noose around her neck, he had ultimate control, like a man out walking his dog.

"All right, sister," he said. "Take my thing out of my pants."

"No," she cried. "I don't want any part of you!"

He cinched the noose a little tighter around her neck. "How many times did I get you off?"

"I—I don't know. I don't even want to think about it."

"SEVEN! Seven times I had you bucking and whooping like some pissed-up rodeo cowboy. Now I'm going to give you a chance to determine which one of us is superior. If you can get me off once, we'll call it even."

"And... and you'll let me go?"

He drew close. She felt his sirocco breath in her ear. "Yes," he whispered.

"And if I don't?"

He pulled the noose a little tighter and grinned.

And though Gretchen found Milburn to be as repulsive as any man (or half man) she'd ever known, the thought of leaving Dan forever, now that they'd been reunited, filled her with a great sadness.

She fished his rod out of his pants for the second time in her life, and began to stroke it slowly. She told herself that it was no different from the countless others she'd worked her magic on—and if she could detach her mind from what her hand and wrist were doing, everything would come out right in the end.

There was a rising chill in the air, and she was thankful that at least now she was fully clothed, and that he hadn't required her to remove them again—and that her fingers were gripping something warm. Gradually, she picked up the pace in hopes that the sensation she was providing would cause him to slacken the already uncomfortable pressure upon her neck.

What she didn't know was that the only way Milburn could get off-- dating back to puberty—was by inhaling the scent of Vicks Vapo-Rub. Initially, he'd applied some of the goop onto his chest to ease the effects of a cold, then absentmindedly touched his penis. Finding the sensation to be pleasurable, he slathered more of the gooey onto his organ—initiating the process that would result in his very first orgasm. Thereafter, whenever he would get a whiff of the pungent stuff, he'd have to leave the area for fear of creaming his jeans. And as good as the little vixen playing a tune on his instrument was—and he had to admit she was—he still wasn't likely to blow any jazz without his gooey.

And now, the question that hung (like other things) in the air: Had Gretchen finally met her match? This was more than a test of will. It was a battle of ideologies.

And so she soldiered on in a valiant attempt to exert her sexual power over him, as he had done to her, to prove that she was at least his equal, and thus indirectly validate her own ideological position.

But Milburn, confident that he could handle all that she could give him, was feeling his oats. YOU CAN'T POP THIS PECKER... YOU CAN'T DETONATE THIS DICK!" he bellowed, his voice echoing through the hills. He followed that up with an amazingly authentic Tarzan yell.

Dan, who had finished watering the foliage in the forest and was heading back to the room, clearly heard the bawling and immediately sensed what was up. Milburn's outburst sent a bolt of fear charging through him. He had the agent's impounded weapon tucked inside his jacket pocket. He'd checked it earlier and was aware that there was only one bullet in the chamber. He drew the gun and clambered up the side of the hill with Harv leading the way. His lungs were burning as he attained the summit. Two figures were dimly visible.

Milburn jerked his head around and saw Dan and the cursed canine charging headlong toward him. "Stay away, Rivers," he warned in an exaggerated James Cagney voice, "or the girl gets it."

What the hell's he saying? Dan thought. I'm the one with the gun. But now he had drawn close enough to assess the nature of the situation.

"Take a good look Rivers... you're whore is choking my chicken—but she's not doing it right, so I'm choking HER!"

Dan watched as Milburn cinched the noose tighter still, and with that Gretchen's fingers relinquished his member. The rope burned into her neck. Her eyes bulged as she clawed at it with both hands in what was now a struggle for her life.

With the clarity of one who is fully awake, perhaps for the first time in his life—Dan saw that his window was no more than a few seconds, and in that time he had to decide whether to attempt to fire his one bullet into the brain of the monster, running the risk of killing Gretchen if the shot was off the mark, or... or what?

Or not.

One moment slid into the next. He couldn't pull the trigger. Still, he had to act. He cued Harv. "Let's get him, boy!"

Milburn tried to fend each of them off with one arm as he kept his grip on the rope with the other. Dan brought the butt of the gun down hard against his skull. Once. Twice. Three limes.

Harv leapt for the most accessible part of the bad guy. He clamped his jaws down in midair and came away with the very tip-top of the head of Milburn's penis. It was just a flesh wound, and Milburn still had plenty of prick left (though in fact he was all prick) but it hurt like hell. He dropped his hands to his crotch.

Gretchen gasped as she sucked in air.

"BASTARD HOUND FROM HELL!" Milburn screamed. Smarting and stinging from both heads at once, he offered little resistance as Dan wrested him to the ground. Gretchen sat on him while her rescuer tied his hands, and this time tightly. They marched him down and loaded him into the back of his panel truck, where Dan discovered a pair of handcuffs. He switched out the rope and fitted Milburn's wrists with the cuffs.

And that was the last time that renegade FBI agent Lawrence Milburn ever bothered them.

As for his injury, the man would find that when it healed, the head of his organ was rounded, just like that of any normal homo sapiens male—which the Bubbas at the prison complex where he was headed would find to be much to their liking.

* * *

Reno and Sondra sat facing each other across the kitchen table in Cletus's cabin. In the main room, Cletus, Sergei, and part of Willie's crew were playing a noisy game of gin rummy. The "Old Bear" had taught his extraterrestrial visitors the basics of the game during the layover time they'd spent waiting for their leader to return. Their dark eyes grew bigger (if that were possible) as each evaluated the cards in his hand.

Earlier, Cletus had received word that the head honcho E.T. would be arriving soon, and that he and his unearthly entourage would be departing forthwith to deposit Reno back into his indigenous era. Sondra looked at Reno with her sad kind eyes.

"I don't know what to say," he said.

"Nothing needs to be said."

Outside the cabin a coyote yipped at the moon.

"Ever wish you could be two places at once?"

"I'm just happy for you… and as for me, well, you made me feel like a twenty-something again."

"Back in the warehouse, Gretchen said I won't remember any of this—but still, maybe I'll find you. After all, we both lived around here. Maybe we'll hook up, you know. We'll be about the same age."

"You're saying that once you get back, from your standpoint, everything that's happened between then and now hasn't happened yet—so anything is still possible?"

"Something like that."

She smiled, and in her expression was all the wisdom of the better part of a lifetime. "If it's meant to be, kid. If it's meant to be."

Fifty-Four

A board op's job is sort of like that of the guy who sells beer and peanuts at the baseball game. You're in the ballpark, but you're not very close to the action. You can tell your friends that you're in radio, if working in radio means babysitting someone else's program—either live or recorded—the main chore being to push some buttons and insert local commercials into the scheduled breaks at the appointed times. That, and sitting around picking your butt.

The board op is one step above the cleaning lady.

And so it was that on New Year's Eve, 1999—arguably the most important night of the century for anyone who is anybody to be SOMEWHERE (meaning other than their place of employment)—Jeremy Higginbottom, computer nerd, part-time student, and full time resident at his parents' place, had, as low man on the KSUK totem pole, drawn the assignment to be holed up inside the station on this momentous occasion.

Jeremy was running the taped replay of a local club hockey game that had taken place three nights ago. Now, the game of hockey is the world's second most boring sport to watch on television (eclipsed only by soccer in the hierarchy of yawners)—the players skating up and down, up and down, with never much of anything actually happening—and when it finally does, you've missed it by looking away for a moment and have to watch the slow motion replay to actually see the puck going into the net, which is anticlimactic, so why bother in the first place? Take this affair and put it on RADIO and you've increased the tedium factor exponentially.

But the sales department had scrounged up a sponsor for the games—a local used sporting goods store operated by the father of one of the players, natch—and as we know, KSUK policy was: If anyone is stupid enough to pay for it, it runs

When the door buzzer sounded, Jeremy had about a minute left in the current spot break before he would have to pot up the audio from the game again. "Shit a brick!" he said. "Who could that be?' Well, he would just run to the door, in case it was Kirshbaum or one of the salespeople who forgot their key, and scamper back to the control room before the end of the break.

Jeremy cracked the door and saw a nondescript looking man--made more so by the baseball cap pulled partially down over his eyes. He hadn't gotten can I help you out of his mouth before the man flashed a badge.

"Agent Sanders—FBI," he said curtly. "We have reason to believe that these premises are in danger."

"Wha—"

"Our intelligence indicates the possibility of a terrorist attack against this station... tonight."

"Shit a brick!" Jeremy repeated.

"I will need to come inside, make a thorough inspection, and secure the premises before calling in the rest of my team."

"Uh... I'll have to call Mister-"

"Mister Fallon has been advised of the situation. Besides, you will not be able to reach him as he is now sequestered at a secure location— for his own protection."

"Time was running out in Jeremy's commercial break. He had to think fast, as he would soon have to dash back into the control room. He was under standing orders not to allow anyone into the building after business hours. But this guy DID know the station owner's name--which, as a rule, was not broadcast over the air, which meant the general public wouldn't know it, which meant that this guy might be who he said he was... and he DID have a badge. "Uh... come on in," he said.

The man made a cursory inspection of the various rooms and offices inside the building—ostensibly to ensure that no bad guys were hiding under the desks or lurking about in the shitter.

He was a thin man with a thin mustache. He had something of a southern, though not a deep south accent. He didn't look like a federal agent to Jeremy, but then, what does one look like— especially if he's undercover? But if the guy had held that badge under his nose for more than a split second, Jeremy might have noticed the words "Dick Tracy" down at the bottom.

When "agent Sanders" had finished casing the joint, he asked to be familiarized with the basic workings of the control board and cassette machines, in case an emergency announcement should need to be broadcast. When Jeremy had explained everything, he was ordered to vacate the premises. It wouldn't do for any civilians to be present during this operation.

"But what about the hockey game?" Jeremy stammered.

The man looked up at the control room clock. It was twenty past eleven. "Is there network programming you can transition into at the bottom of the hour? Something self-contained that will run itself— make its own gravy?"

"Yeah... but the game won't be over by then."

The man put his hand on Jeremy's shoulder. "Son, do you REALLY think anybody cares?"

"Uh... no," the board op said with a guilty little laugh. "Nobody but the sponsors, and they're probably drunk by now."

Jeremy took off, thinking he'd done his civic duty, remembering the fed man's admonishment not to breathe a word of this to anyone.

When he heard the kid's car pull out of the lot, the stranger set about his duties. When his work out at the transmitter was done, and his preparations inside the station completed, he popped the prerecorded tape that was inside his shirt pocket into the cassette player, faded the network down, and pressed the play button on the machine. Fifteen minutes, timed out exactly. Surely his last fifteen minutes of fame.

It was 11:45 p.m.

The stranger sprinted to his vehicle, revved it up, and proceeded to get the hell out of Dodge, as his disembodied voice went out over the airwaves:

In the beginning was the word. It wasn't a bad word—like shit, piss, or fart No, it was a good word. Hence the phrase, "What's the good word?" which was first spoken by Adam or one of those early guys. Then the word became amplified… modulated… and broadcast all over the land—and everybody knew, at least during the sixties, that the BIRD was the word.

But we're getting ahead of ourselves. Inevitably, the commercial announcement was born, which strung a whole bunch of words together, most of which were pure bullshit. Soon, it was my product is better than yours… three out of four doctors recommend Chesterfields… you'll wonder where the yellow went when you brush your teeth with Pepsodent.

But ultimately, this kind of nonsense wasn't good enough. And so, the fine print was born. The fine print laid out all the important details they didn't tell you up front in the commercial—just too small for anyone to actually read. The purpose of the fine print was to put one over on the dumb asses. Didn't have your glasses on, Granny? Or didn't have time to read those tiny words in the two seconds they were flashed upon the TV screen? Too bad! We've got your signature on this piece of paper and you're now obligated to pay through the nose for the rest of your wretched life!

And now we have the radio version of the fine print, which is the guy at the end of the commercial who talks so fast you'd swear he was speaking a foreign language. Yes, they're playing a kind of shell game with you—and it's all legal.

Finally, some genius determined that if thirty seconds of blowing smoke up the public's ass was good, thirty MINUTES would be even better—thus, the INFOMERCIAL was born.

In another part of town, an elderly couple, Dorothy and Phil, were dozing off periodically in their effort to make it to midnight for their annual New Year's eve toast. KSUK was tuned in on the radio—for background noise mainly—since they didn't care for those rock 'n' roll countdown shows on the tube. But when a voice Dorothy was unfamiliar with came on, she pricked up her ears. Giving her husband a shove, she said, "Wake up, Phil, and listen to this man on the radio."

"Er... what is it, Dot—some new preacher on there?"

"Well, if it is, he's sure got a peculiar way about 'im. Usin' language I've never heard the likes of on the radio... listen!

Mike Fallon is a name most of you are probably not familiar with. But he owns this dubious excuse for a radio station, and others like it around the country. Mike Fallon is the one who said: Why not create an entire station full of thirty minute horse shit pitches for products, masquerading as interviews and talk shows, along with lunatic right-wing evangelists and various and sundry other types of programming of a highly questionable nature...

Phil said, "I heard worse than that on some of them FM stations."

"Phil, no!" said his wife.

"Why, I even heard 'em say PUSSY once!"

"My lord, Phil—why you listenin' to such filth?"

"Now, Dot... I was just rotatin' the dial, lookin' for some Lawrence Welk music."

An entire station given over to the vain and the delusional—like its creator, the notorious PUSSY HOUND, Mike Fallon—the embodiment of greed, who thinks he can, and should, have it all...

This last fusillade of filth was too much for Dorothy, who clutched her chest and said, "Oh... my heart... get me my nitro... get me my heart medicine quick!"

Simultaneously, the residents of the few households that had KSUK tuned in as an innocuous alternative to the glitzy TV specials began to turn their heads—and turn up the volume: They called their friends and told them to tune in the guy who was ranting on 690. Who was he? A new charismatic preacher? Those who'd been notified began to notify others, and the process was repeated, until KSUK's listening audience became the largest in the city that evening... for a few minutes, anyway.

Make no mistake—there are consequences to all of our actions, and anyone who thinks differently is blind. I AM ONE OF THE CONSEQUENCES OF MIKE FALLON'S ACTIONS...

Jeremy, listening on the car radio, heard the network programming he'd put on the air just prior to departing give way to "agent Sanders" rant. With growing alarm, he realized that he had made a grievous mistake.

Possessing no cell phone, and still in the middle of the no man's land between the station and the edge of the city, Jeremy did the only thing he could do to try to save his own ass—which was to cut a sharp U in the middle of the road, head back to the station, and try to play hero.

As he sped back toward the studios, Jeremy envisioned removing the tire iron from his trunk and walloping the interloper over the head with it. He'd never been a violent kid, but like most nerds, he was prone to all manner of secret fantasies—some of which involved the revenge torture and mutilation of classmates he didn't care for.

What Jeremy didn't know, as he turned onto the last half mile stretch of dirt road leading to the station in the final sixty seconds of the millennium, was that the intruder was, at that moment, tearing down 1-10 east, already on the outskirts of town and not looking back— anticipating the stroke of midnight and murmuring, "This one's for you, ol' buddy."

The second hand made its last ever rotation around the face of the control room clock as the tape played to its conclusion: *You never know which mangy cur you kicked around will come back to bite you on the ass... KICK OUT THE JAMS, MOTHERFUCKERS!*

There were two seconds of dead silence.

Then, a bright flash near the base of the transmitter tower, followed by a deafening blast. There's heavy metal, and then there's HEAVY METAL. The tower—like a rocket self-destructing on its launch pad—crashed to the ground in a thunderous, disintegrating slow motion swan dive—Mike Fallon's tallest and firmest erection keeled over dead.

Jeremy stomped on the brake and his car fishtailed to a halt, stopping short of the entrance to the station parking lot, but close enough to see, hear, and feel what came next—the second explosion that rocked the earth as it blasted out the windows and blew the roof off the building that, only a moment ago, had housed the KSUK studios.

"SHIT A BRICK!" He dove for the floorboard on the passenger side as debris rained down on his vehicle's roof. Shards of glass. A mangled piece of the frame that held the photo of Mike Fallon's wife and kids that had occupied a place of prominence atop his desk. Part of a toilet seat.

Minutes later, Jeremy too felt the need for speed, burning up the freeway in his somewhat battered and dented automobile—high tailing it out of town.

And all of those people listening when the KSUK signal suddenly went dead looked at each other knowingly and said, "Y2K, Phil... Y2K, Bernice... Y2K, Maude...

As to whom would become the prime suspect in the bombing... well, that had to do with the nature of the radio business, and specifically the nature of Mike Fallon and his ilk. Over the years there'd been so many hirelings who were unceremoniously booted out the door (at each of his stations), and many more who left voluntarily, but not amicably, that there really was no single disgruntled former employee to focus upon. Especially not Jack Davis because, as is the case with many wheeler-dealers who see only interchangeable components rather than human beings, Mike Fallon didn't even remember him.

Fifty-Five

It had turned into a party of sorts—New Year's Eve as well as a sendoff for Reno. Once agent Milburn had been taken into custody, and Willie, Dan, Gretchen, and Harv had arrived back at Cletus's place, the wine flowed freely. There were toasts to Reno's new old life. Another toast to the reunited couple. A toast to Willie's bunghole and the devastating laser shot that had emanated from it.

Amidst the merriment, Dan grew quiet as he considered the state of his (re)union with Gretchen. Thinking about a possible future together, he realized that the basic bone of contention between them had not been resolved. Would things begin to deteriorate again, as each of them took up the hard line positions they'd adopted before the breakup? Were they fooling themselves, when perhaps they were just two people who were ultimately incompatible?

Sensing the shift in mood, Gretchen took him aside. "Listen," she said. "I don't want to eat meat anymore."

"Uh... okay," he replied, taken aback by the sudden pronouncement.

"And I don't want to BEAT meat anymore either. Being holed up in that horrible warehouse gave me time to think. I will find an assistant—ideally another hybrid who will recognize the importance of my work. A dedicated female—single, of course—who won't mind the hands on aspect of human sperm collection."

He looked at her then with tenderness, and in his eyes she saw the whole of their future together.

"Are you sure?" he said. "Because you don't need to change for me..."

"Of this you can be certain... there will be only one penis between us. I still believe, however, that our mission is a noble one, and that someday we will succeed in breeding the primitive instincts of hatred and violence out of the human race."

There was a pregnant pause. Then Dan said, "I'm happy for Reno, and that he won't become an old fart before his time."

Gretchen's expression changed. She looked like the little girl who's been caught with her hand down her underpants. She looked around to see where the others were, then leaned in close to him. "I—I manipulated the truth... a little. I don't really know what the effects of being instantaneously transported thirty years into the future would be. I was being a little fanciful with the story about Reno's premature aging."

Dan was incredulous. "Why... why did you do this?!!"

"I knew that Reno was lost, and that he needed to go back home--to the place and the people he knew. So I gave him a little added incentive."

He stared at her for a protracted moment. His head fell to his chest. Gretchen had known nothing of Maya, nor of the plan he had shared with Reno that night in the desert. Or did she?

According to the timeline as Dan had pieced it together, she'd invented her little story before locating Reno in Sedona. Was it just possible, though, that she'd read either or both of their minds--her little fabrication effecting the twofold purpose of sending the right one back and keeping the other one put?

When he raised his head he was smiling. It was a question for another time. "You told me yourself that it was a better era," she continued. What was that phrase you used?"

"A kinder, gentler time?"

"Yes, that's it."

He looked off into an imaginary distance. "Yes," he said. "In some ways... it was."

They glanced up to see Willie standing there. "Time to send our boy on his way," the diminutive one said.

One by one, Willie's crew filed into Cletus's garage and took up their positions aboard Nelly Belle. Everyone that was left embraced Reno in turn. Willie was last to board the craft. He turned and saluted his terrestrial comrades. "We'll be back on occasion," he said, "and next time I'm going to kick your asses at poker!"

He looked at Cletus and shrugged.

Cletus looked round at the others. "You know, we have to give this thing a shove."

His statement was met with an exaggerated chorus of groans, as everyone lined up behind the saucer. They put some muscle into it and wheeled the silver spacecraft into the open.

As they did, Cletus, the longtime recluse, felt his heart begin to open, and he was suddenly gratified to have the camaraderie of friends.

They stood back and watched her take off--straight up, until she looked to be the size of a pie plate ascending into the heavens.

"Godspeed, Reno Vegas," Sondra whispered. Instinctively, she clasped the hand of the person next to her, which was Sergei. As she did so, she nearly jumped. There was electricity there—the kind of feeling she'd experienced on only rare occasions.

Sergei felt it as well.

She looked up at him from the corner of her eye. Oh no, she thought… here we go again.

Oh YEAH! Sergei said to himself. Here we go again.

Fifty-Six

Jackie waved her free hand in front of his face. "Wake UP, Reno," she said.

"Uh... I'm here," he said with a start. "I'm here."

"Where'd you go, silly?"

"I—I don't know. It was like I checked out for a while."

"1 think you were dreaming."

"Mmm... maybe so."

They were sitting in his cherry red '66 Mustang convertible—parked on a lonely desert road. It was a clear night with a myriad of stars peppering the sky.

"Lookit this thing in my hand," she said. "Some catch of the day. It shrivels up any more, I might as well throw it back."

Reno glanced down at his wilting member ensconced inside Jackie's fist. He looked up at her face. She wasn't bad. Why hadn't he seen it before? Sure, her nose took up a little too much space in the middle, but otherwise there was nothing wrong with her. Twenty-two years old and actually kind of cute.

He felt himself beginning to respond again in her accomplished grip.

"Ooh, that's better," she said. "Want to get out of the car so's I can milk you underneath the Milky Way, like you always say?"

Reno looked up at the sky. "Naw… we ain't gonna do that."

"What? Why not?"

"Well, 'cause I'm gonna STICK IT TO YA, that's why!'

"Oh Reno, you're crazy. NOBODY fucks Jack-Off Jackie."

"It's high time somebody did. Get your fanny in that back seat, gal."

"You mean it Reno? Really?"

And before he could utter another sound, Jackie dove over the seat and proceeded to remove her knickers. Reno crawled in back with her. There was a blanket on the floor and he used it to cover the both of them from head to toe. He didn't know why, but he had this funny feeling that somehow, everything was about to change.

A minute later, an extraterrestrial craft passed overhead. It was a rogue bunch, cruising for hapless earthlings to abduct. But, detecting only what looked like an abandoned vehicle in the area, they continued on their way—leaving just the cool night breeze and a faint but steady sound of creaking springs that blended in with the song of the crickets.

Acknowledgements

Many thanks and a debt of gratitude to my editor (and poet extraordinaire), Marian Kent.

A salute to the creative brilliance of John Connolly, who has proven that you can judge a book by its cover.

A shout out to C. Kossack, vagabond princess and source of unlimited inspiration.

And with fond remembrance of Lloyd Oakley McDole, my high school English teacher—who intercepted one of my nasty little poems as it was being passed from classmate to sniggering classmate—looked at it… began to laugh… then, red-faced, went on a half-hour tirade about how SUCH TRASH WAS THE PRODUCT OF A SICK MIND! It was then and there that I began to entertain the idea that maybe I could become a writer!

About the Author

Tim Schaefer spent way too many years as a rock-n-roll radio deejay—"town to town, up and down the dial"—yet somehow survived. He resides in southern Arizona, where he feels right at home with the vermin and the varmints of the desert.